CHASE
FOR YOUR LIFE

CHASE
FOR YOUR LIFE

DOUGLAS
ROBERTS

Lieutenant-Colonel Bernard Utting OBE
Commissioned into the Royal Engineers in 1939, decommissioned
from the XIV 'forgotten army' in December 1945.

Foreword

There are many reasons why the Second World War ever took place, but few dispute that it was German aggression that provoked Britain and her allies into declaring war in the early days of September 1939. The German war machine had been preparing for this since the mid-1930s, and consequentially had the most modern and well-equipped military machine in the entire world. Confident that nobody would be able to stand in their way, the Germans invaded France in May 1940, and such was their competence that they surprised and surrounded the British Expeditionary Force of nearly 400,000 men. The infamous Dunkirk evacuation is a shining example of what the British can achieve when their backs are against the wall, and the German army, quite rightly at the time, had the arrogance to assume that they could conquer the rest of Europe; and they almost did. The British were outmatched by the Germans in virtually every department and in May 1940, when our stories begin, the continent of Europe was quickly coming under the control of The Third Reich, complete with their atrocious acts.

The powerful German Propaganda Ministry was very active for several years leading up to 1939 and successfully managed to deceive and mislead their people about opposing nations to such an extent that the German army simply marched across national borders and claimed countries and regions for themselves. They couldn't conceive that a single country could offer any sort of protracted resistance, so the Germans merely marched through Belgium, attacking and sweeping all before them in one of their now infamous Blitzkriegs and carried on into France. Lightning (blitz) war (krieg) indeed.

Newly commissioned Second Lieutenant Stock of the Royal Engineers, commonly known as the Sappers, was not long out of officer training corps and cast into this toxic scenario where there was often a fine line between life and death.

Chapter 1

Escape

Paris May 1940

The brothel keeper's wife was starting to worry about her reputation as she faced up to the two burly types in front of her. It was her kudos that was at stake. She thought she knew everyone worth knowing from the local police prefecture and could certainly name, if she ever decided to be indiscreet, several of the more senior officers, but these two claimed to be from the Interior Inspectorate and outside of her sphere of influence. Nevertheless, she would have a word with Claude, a sympathetic Inspector in the 9th arrondissement, and see if he could find out if the Interior Ministry was going to be taking a closer interest in her dealings with some of her more sensitive clients.

A third man descended the narrow staircase, briefly shook his head towards the two brutes, and continued out of the front door that led indirectly onto rue Cauchois in the Pigalle Quarter, the red-light district of Paris. The smaller of the two men took half a pace nearer and looked down on his prey.

"Remember, Madame, that these two convicts are known for their subtlety and even someone in your profession can be deceived." He continued to maintain an air of officialdom despite suspecting that the madame knew that they were not from any police department. "I'll leave a man across the street just in case."

"Just in case what?"

"Just in case they should appear. After all, we don't want any unnecessary violence, do we? And we are here for your protection.

They are described as being very dangerous.”

"You mean just in case you think I'm lying.”

"Think what you like, Madame, but we will catch these two criminals and if we find that they have been here, we will make sure you know the meaning of cooperation." He briefly lifted his hat at the same time as smiling the way a shark seems to smile just before it devours its meal.

They had gone only a few paces outside before Madame frowned. Up to that point she had portrayed her kindly face, the one reserved for customers and officials, but now she was angry. They hadn't even offered her any money, only threats, and had her husband not gone out to visit one of his associates… Well, she could imagine the fracas that would have taken place. Perhaps it was for the best he was out of the way for the moment, as it would have only ended up with some of the furniture being damaged. As she climbed the stairs, she didn't think that any of her regulars had seen or heard the incident, but one or two might have been a little disgruntled if they'd noticed the door to their temporary love nest being briefly opened. She saw Monsieur Carven adjusting his tie as he emerged from Sylfie's room, and was deciding what to say about the intrusion, but instead he just smiled at her as he held out the usual 40 francs and continued down the corridor.

"Tomorrow?" she called after him.

"Not tomorrow but maybe Thursday. Au revoir."

Sylfie's door was still open, so she entered. There was an unwritten rule in the house that if a door was closed, one didn't open it. Sylfie looked up from massaging her knees.

"I like him, but it's a bit rough on my knees and it's starting to wear the carpet just there."

Madame looked down at part of the compacted carpet and ignored the suggestion that a new rug might soon be needed.

"Did you notice anything different today?" She wanted to know how much of a disturbance the third man had caused when he looked into every room.

Sylfie ceased her rubbing and looked thoughtfully at her employer. "Should I have done?" Then it dawned on her that Madame might be looking for an excuse to get rid of her; and it showed on her face. "Oh, no… no… no… no! I am not too old, and they do keep coming back to me." She was only 28, and they both knew there was only a couple of years left in her before her body started to reflect the ravages of a constant stream of men.

"Relax. I was just wondering if you heard anything out of the ordinary, like a door closing."

A look of relief crossed Sylfie's face. "No, nothing."

Madame looked at her watch. "You've got a spare hour or so before your lunchtime appointment, so you may as well freshen yourself up." She turned to leave but had second thoughts. "And while you're at it, make sure you've got enough perfume this time. You know what he's like. Oh, I just want to check the water tank upstairs, so keep an eye on the counter for me, will you? Gabi will be done soon and he's to pay 55 Francs this time. Now, if you don't mind…"

She left Sylfie prettying herself with a brush and dressing at the same time, continued down the dog-legged corridor and climbed two further flights of stairs up to the top floor, noting that the bed in Astino's room was sounding a bit rusty. Right at the end of a dingy corridor hung a full-size painting of a gentleman astride a horse, sporting a decent erection. She pushed gently on the upper right-hand side of the frame then swung it back on its hinges to reveal a cubicle not much bigger than a broom cupboard.

"So far, you two are more trouble than you are worth. You may as well come out as they've gone….. for the moment."

The slightly smaller bespectacled man was fluent in French and understood her colloquial Parisian dialect, unlike the obvious-looking Englishman opposite him, to whom he gestured to likewise stretch his legs.

"I'm not used to this either, but I'm sure my chief will make it worthwhile. Believe me when I say I don't like small rooms. How did they know where to come?"

"They didn't. They were just fishing, and I expect they'll be fishing elsewhere for the rest of the day so you may as well take over one of the spare rooms until Yves comes back." Madame retraced a few steps and opened a door into small room with a typical French mansard-type window that overlooked that part of Paris. "You'll have to share the bed, though, but don't let that worry you… we're used to that round here." The grin on her face said it all.

The staining on the striped mattress attested to its usage and, for the first time since their arrival, Madame heard the Englishman speak, not that she understood what he was saying other than the word 'please.' She'd had few dealings with Englishmen but just enough to pick up the occasional word, and now had the chance to look more closely at the foreigner that had come to them, accompanied by the official looking type from the British embassy. He was a tallish lanky man, plainly more suited to working in an office or the like and had an air about him that portrayed nervousness, but he had a kindly looking face and so far had done exactly what he had been told to do.

"Ask her if she's got anything to eat. Please. And where's the toilet?"

Once the translations were made, the Englishman trotted out of the room, still clutching his valise.

"Even if you knew what was going on I don't suppose you'd tell me, would you?" Now Madame was fishing.

Simon had introduced himself a couple of years ago, when he had taken the job as third attaché to the British embassy in Paris. His predecessor had told him to visit Madame d'Esteau's parlour, as the family that owned it had strong sympathies - and indeed connections – in the right places and was an excellent source of information. Their relationship had been purely platonic but, however hard he tried, Simon had been unable to discover what those connections were, other than it was something to do with her husband Yves. Still, he had soon found out that they were willing to help in all sorts of ways, including an endless supply of manpower whenever anything clandestine came along. Right now, and with the German threat, those clandestine operations were coming thick and fast.

"Not a chance, and no, I don't know what's going on, only that we've got to get this chap to Orly Airport pronto and get him on a plane without the Germans finding out."

"Ha! That's a joke. They seem to be able to find out what's happening before we even make our own minds up. There's swarms of them out there. Who is he, anyway?"

Simon thought carefully before replying. "I don't think you ought to know that, just in case, but someone in London wants him back badly."

"You mean just in case the Germans do manage to capture Paris and torture me to tell them, eh?"

Simon didn't have to respond as the look on his face gave away the answer. "Yes. Something like that."

"Is he important enough for a thousand francs?"

"A thousand?"

"You said he's important, so a thousand ought to do it. Ok?"

"Ok. I'll pop over in the next few days."

From their previous meetings, Madame knew he'd be good for it. "I suppose if the Nazis do get here, you lot will disappear off safely to England and leave us to deal with the bastards."

Now it was Simon's turn and with a wry smile he retorted, "Somebody's got to do it and anyway, just think how rich you'll become."

"I know, I know. Milk them while you can." The rhythmic squeaking in the background suddenly ceased. "That reminds me, I must do something about Astino's bed springs." They both heard a door close somewhere in the building, but it was only Madame who recognised it from the creak. "That may be Yves. You wait here and keep an eye on our English friend, and I'll go and see what his news is."

Alone for the moment, Simon turned his attention to the window, rested his hands on the ledge, and listened to the familiar noises of Parisians going about their daily business while he mused over the forthcoming problem of getting Rutherford to Orly airfield unseen. Madame was right in that there were swarms of Germans and their Vichy sympathisers roaming the streets, and they seemed to be operating with impunity and becoming bolder every day. The German war machine was closing in on Paris and his chief had, only this morning, told him that it was just a matter of days before Paris fell; it was likely that they would be ordered back to London by the end of the week. In the meantime, his task for today had been to pick up Rutherford from the Hotel Bristol and get him on the plane that had been specially dispatched from England. Preferably without the Germans finding out. It was this last part that was now causing considerable problems; only when he eventually found Rutherford hiding in his own bedroom wardrobe, did he begin to appreciate how badly the Germans also wanted him. He'd passed three of them in the lobby and recognised one of the bully boys; if he brought Rutherford out through the main entrance, they would simply overpower him and kidnap his charge. He also suspected that they would be guarding the rear entrance, so he had had a discreet word with one of the concierges with whom he had had dealings in the past, slipped him a few francs, and smuggled Rutherford out through the kitchen dressed in a chef's outfit. Unfortunately, the route back to his car was blocked by yet more Germanic types, obviously on the lookout, hence his only other immediate option had been to head for Madame's on foot.

Looking for inspiration, he leaned out of the window and gazed down at the street below just as a baker's van pulled up. He considered that if Yves knew the delivery man, perhaps they could use that method. With Orly being over ten miles away to the south, one thing was certain: they would need transport.

"What are you looking at?"

He nearly jumped out of his skin as he had not heard Rutherford return.

"Bloody hell! Don't do that again. Creeping up on someone like that's going to give me a heart attack."

"Sorry. What are you looking at?"

Simon thought he looked a little less worried, but he still had his oversized briefcase clutched across his chest. He didn't want to give away the fact that he hadn't yet a clear idea as to how they were going to reach Orly but was relying upon Yves to come up with something. Perhaps a baker's van might not be such a bad idea after all.

"Oh, just looking over the sights and sounds of Paris. I fell in love with the city when my parents brought me here when I was just a lad, but it's the smell of the cooking that I really adore. Here, see what I mean." He sidestepped so that Rutherford could stand by the window and appreciate the vantage point. "If you lean out a little and look to the right you can see the Eiffel Tower."

Rutherford duly obliged, changing the grip on his case to his right hand. He'd seen the huge tower before, but it was still an awe-inspiring sight, despite it being two or three miles away. "I suppose we just have to wait until Yves gets back?" He had turned to face Simon and now sat down on the bed.

"Madame's gone to find him now. Thinks he's just returned." Simon mused a little before posing the question, "I know it's not my business, but what you've got in that case, is it really that important?"

The silence between them, coupled with the eye contact said it all, but Rutherford replied anyway, "It is. Up to this morning I thought it was going to be easy getting this back to England, but then Jerry turned up and it all changed. Obviously, more than just a handful of people now know about this, but not from me they don't. You see, I'm not the person they think I am."

Rutherford watched the frown develop on Simon's forehead and could see him struggling with this latest snippet of information, so continued, "I'm not about to be indiscreet to you or anyone else but those chaps you spotted at the Bristol were probably from then same bunch who were following Miltz and took him away. He's the chap I was picking this lot up from." He patted his case. "Just after I collected this from him and returned to my room, I heard a commotion in the corridor. I opened the door just enough to see them strong-arming him towards the lift and decided it wouldn't be long before they came after me. I wasn't too sure about you when I spotted you searching my room from my vantage point in the wardrobe, but somehow you didn't look like their type. By the way, how did you know I was hiding in the wardrobe?"

Simon wondered if he ought to tell Rutherford the truth, because it was almost blind luck and desperation that had steered him towards the only remaining place in the room that he hadn't searched. He tilted his head slightly and with a wink replied, "Now, that's one of my little secrets."

They both heard Madame's footfall on the stairs before they saw her, and when she did come into sight saw that she was holding a bundle of clothing. She held them out for Rutherford but addressed Simon, "Tell him to put these on. We're going to smuggle him out as a bakers' mate in a van. Here, here's yours!"

"The one that's just pulled up?"

"Yes. Yves will drive him to the airfield in his cousin's van and won't have any problem getting through the gates as they're used to a delivery on a daily basis. He tells me they're rather desperate to get hold of your Englishman and they know he's somewhere in the district." She watched Simon struggle into a long white jacket over his suit and don a crumpled bakers' cap. "He must be important for them to be taking so much interest in him because there's dozens of them out there looking for him. Oh, God. He doesn't really look like a baker, does he?"

They both stood back and looked at Simon who had finished buttoning the well-worn coat.

"Can't you throw some flour over him or something? Make him look a little pasty."

"Do I look like a baker's wife?"

Simon really did look pathetic and certainly anything but a baker as he stood there now holding the case to his chest again.

"It'll help if he can hold his case flat and cover it with a cloth, like it was a tray of buns. Have you got one?"

"Follow me." Madame took them down one flight of stairs and into her own well-appointed bedroom. "Try this." She had taken a pillowcase from one of the drawers. The frills gave away what it really was but, at a glance, it would suffice.

"And how about a little puff?" She went over to her dresser and selected a tin of white powder and a brush. Once she had finished with Simon he was starting to look a little more realistic; there was even some flour-looking substance down his black trousers and on his shoes. She opened a cupboard door on which was fixed a full-length mirror and steered Rutherford in front of it.

"What do you think?"

"Better," replied Simon. "Just don't ask him to speak, that's all. How do I look?" Somehow, Simon seemed to match the appearance of someone connected to a bakery.

"What happens if they ask me what's under the cloth?" asked Rutherford as he indicated to his tray.

"Don't say anything," they emphatically retorted in unison. Madame immediately understood.

"Quickly now, downstairs. Yves will be eager to get going."

On the way down the stairs, Simon suggested Rutherford practiced holding the case a little more level as though he were actually carrying buns, but then he looked more like an altar boy. Madame led them towards the back of the building, opened an outside door and sneaked a look up and down the street, before turning to Simon.

"Yves is standing by the van about ten meters away outside the bakery on the other side of the road. Let him know we're ready. It's probably best if you just saunter up as though you've just delivered some bread. There's a couple of thugs dressed in their usual dark suits down the far end, but it looks like they're not paying too much attention to what's happening in this direction. I couldn't see any the other way, so you ought to manage it. I'll hold English here until you give me the nod. OK?"

Simon finished lighting a roll up. "Right."

"Bonne chance."

Simon had taken three just three paces from the door when he made eye contact with Yves and concentrated on walking nonchalantly towards him. He could see the two thugs at the end of the street talking to each other and considered that they were far enough away not to be able to recognise facial features accurately, but carried on with the charade just in case there were others lurking elsewhere.

It was Yves who spoke first, "Ready?"

Simon had only met him on two occasions before - and then only in passing - but instant recognition was enough this time; the faintest of nods was enough for Yves. Simon went to get into the Citroen van, turned, stared at the doorway he had just come from and nodded, but rather than get into the van, he bent down and pretended to tie his shoelace while keeping an eye on Rutherford's progress. He groaned. His entire demeanour, accentuated by his ungainly gait, shouted to anybody who may have been looking at him, that he was masquerading. Simon could not tie his shoelace for any longer and stood up, covertly glancing down the far end of the street, praying that the thugs were not paying any attention. His anxiety increased when he saw that they had been joined by a third man who was gesticulating in their direction.

"Get in - quick!"

Rutherford ignored the advice he had been given earlier about keeping the case flat well before he squeezed himself into the small van and found himself squashed between the two of them even further as Simon got in beside him and slammed the door shut.

"Go!"

Yves had already started the engine but now, with the extra weight, had to rev the engine more than usual and let the clutch out more slowly, all of which attracted more attention than was expected. The normally underpowered Citroen eventually gathered pace as Yves awkwardly worked the gear lever protruding from the dashboard between Rutherford's knees. Simon soon realised that Yves was addressing him and swearing at the same time.

"Is this guy a natural prat or is he working for the Boche? Have a look out of the window when I make this turning and see if those jokers are after us."

They all swayed together when Yves wrenched the wheel round to take the sharp right-hand turning down a narrow street.

"Didn't look like it. Here, watch out, there's more of them."

The Germans were easy to spot as another pair emerged from a doorway besides a fromagerie, and Yves had to slow down to go round a collection of small urns that had temporarily been left in the street. This provided an opportunity for one of them to peer through the van window as they passed at little more than walking pace. Perhaps it was the eye contact that gave them away. While Yves and Simon were both versed in managing to look indifferent, the opposite was true of Rutherford; he couldn't help but look. However, by the time he was recognised, they were past the pair and turning onto a far busier tree-lined Boulevard where they were able to pick up greater speed.

"That chap looked at me as though he recognised me," Rutherford exclaimed.

"Why do you say that?" replied Simon.

"Well, it was just the way he looked at me. Do you think they have a photograph of me?"

"Let's hope not. You probably match their description, that's all. It's about an hour to Orly. If he did recognise you, that'll give them plenty of time to telephone ahead." Simon related Rutherford's observation to Yves and the two of them spoke across Rutherford as they made their way over the Seine on the most famous of the bridges over the river, the Pont Neuf.

"He says that, even if they do telephone ahead, they won't dare to block the airfield entrance. Anyway, we're not going through the main gates, we're going in the tradesmen's entrance. We've then got to look out for a Hawker Hart that's standing by for you." He didn't add that he hoped that the pilot was not having lunch somewhere.

"What about passport and customs formalities? Won't they want to look at my case and check my passport?"

"No. My chief at the embassy told me that that had all been taken care of. It's surprising how cooperative the French can be when it suits them, and I suspect there'll be someone from their Deuxième Bureau close by."

"What's the Deuxième Bureau?"

"That's their equivalent of our own military security. Once we arrive at the plane, all you have to do is get on it and the pilot will do the rest. OK?"

Rutherford was feeling chuffed that so much trouble was being taken to get him and his case back to England, but knowing how important it was, felt that it was justified. He was still a worried man and didn't smile, even though the suburbs of Paris were beginning to thin out. Now and again, Simon would lean out of the window to see if they were being followed but it was apparent that they were not, as the old Napoleonic A7 road that was once the main link to Lyon in the south east of the country, was mostly straight. With Paris disappearing into the distance behind them, they followed a line of cars, all loaded with luggage and crammed with household belongings. Yves briefly pointed at the one in front with his finger.

"Looks like the better off are deserting Paris for their country estates. You probably didn't hear as I've only picked this one up a short while ago myself, but the Germans have just taken Saint-Quentin. There's only the Armée du Nord between us and them. Your English army looks like it's going to be cut off around Dunkirk."

Simon knew better than to ask how Yves had got this latest news before he himself had heard it. "Do you think they'll stand?"

Yves somehow managed a typical gallic shrug, despite being squashed. "Our masters in Paris tell us they will push them back to the Maginot line within days, but we all know that the Armée du

Nord is made up of a bunch of retiring veterans who struggle to fit into their uniforms, so I suspect we'll soon all be under the jackboot. One of my uncles is an adjutant in the signals corps and he's nearly sixty. He can tell you how to send any message you want using flags but ask him to operate a radio and he wouldn't even know how to turn it on. No. Our only hope was your British expeditionary force but they're now surrounded and stuck against the Channel ports. Perhaps you ought to return to England with our friend here?" He took time to watch Simon's reaction.

"It's a tempting thought, but I think I had better return to Paris with you. You'll stay of course?"

The road ahead was suddenly clear as the car in front half pulled over for no apparent reason and Yves had to test the van's rusty suspension as he swerved around it.

"Of course, we'll stay. Business has been a bit slack of late but when the Germans arrive, I'm hoping we'll have more customers than we know what to do with. Besides which, someone's got to keep you British informed as to what's going on in Paris."

Simon thought he would mention to his chief that maybe Yves ought to be given a radio before they abandoned Paris; no doubt he'd be given the job of delivering it without being seen. This was just one of the reasons why he had joined the Service: it was a little more than run-of-the-mill paperwork. They continued in silence for the next twenty minutes, the squeaks and rattles of the van, coupled with the noise of the asthmatic engine and their rather uncomfortable posture, made it a rather unpleasant journey, but they all knew it wouldn't be long now.

"We're going to pass the main entrance on the left in a minute. See if you can spot any of our friends waiting."

As they passed a small spur road that led to Orly Aerodrome, Simon craned his neck to look at the not very impressive, gated entrance. "There's a drab looking saloon waiting outside the gates but I can't tell what make at this distance, and I can't see if there's anyone in it… No, wait a minute… I can see the outline of a hat…

Yes, that's them. Don't slow down!"

Yves didn't, and it was no more than a couple of minutes before he turned off down a side track just before they entered a wood. "Let's hope they're not here." He had to slow to negotiate a large pothole that was threatening to bisect the entire rather loose tarmac, but then turned and followed the perimeter fence.

"There's the gates. Here, hold your case flat and make sure it's covered." He shifted a little so that Rutherford could comply.

Simon was peering through the wire fence trying to spot the Hawker with British markings, but there were some hangars in the way and he didn't get a good look until they pulled up. He noticed that, mercifully, the gates were not closed, only manned by one officious person armed with no more than a clip board. Yves waved and half hung his head out of the window as they stopped, chatted away for a few seconds, and then carried on through the gates.

"That was too easy," remarked Simon.

"Maurice and I go back a long way. Besides which, one of his cousins used to work with us."

Simon was about to ask what he meant by 'work' when it dawned on him and decided not to comment.

"Is that it?" Rutherford had been trying to make himself taller so as to increase his field of vision.

"Looks like it. When we get there, you wait in the van while I go and find the pilot."

A quarter of a mile away, waiting outside one of the larger open hangars, stood a sleek looking biplane with the tell-tale red, white, and blue circle half way down the fuselage, declaring its origin as British. Yves didn't need a translation and steered the van towards it across the grass, and quite sensibly parked close to the hangar. As Simon got out and disappeared through the cavernous entrance, Yves, while rolled up a cigarette, while looking up and down the line of hangars assessing to assess if anyone looked out of place but there was only one mechanic working on the tail fin of a decrepit-looking aircraft that looked as though it has last seen action in the previous war, twenty twenty-five years earlier. He was nearly at the end of his cigarette and starting to worry, when Simon and the obvious pilot emerged, obvious because of his flight suit. Both Yves and Rutherford got out of the van which shuffled a couple of inches higher with the weight loss.

Simon made the introductions. "This is Lieutenant Mallow and he'll be taking you from here."

"David to you and my friends, and before you ask, yes, I am often called Marsh, but I can assure you I'm not a soft touch." The pilot's wide grin underlined a mop of fair hair that was clearly too long for regulation length, but it suited him, and they shook hands.

"Robert Rutherford - Rubby to my friends. When do we leave?"

"Right away - I gather you're a VIP with an army of Krauts after you, so please do get in. No, not that side, that's mine, go round the back. Can you strike the prop for me?" he asked Simon and pointed to the propeller.

Simon hadn't had the honour of helping to start an aeroplane before and Mallow had to show him what to do, while Rutherford struggled up into the cockpit.

"You turn the prop slowly this way, always this way, and feel when the engine tries to resist. Once you feel that, hold the prop where it is and don't turn it further until I shout 'contact.' When I do, you pull it down as hard as you can and step back smartly, unless you want a close haircut. Understand? Here, I'll help you through the first part."

With Mallow's hand on the prop at the same time as his, Simon felt the propeller turn easily, but then it cushioned to a stop. "That's the position. Now don't forget to keep your hands out of the way once it starts."

It took a couple of minutes before Mallow leaned out of the window. "Contact!"

Simon yanked the propeller down as hard as he could. He had hardly regained his balance and taken a step back when the engine fired into life.

"Thanks for that. See you back in England sometime," Mallow waved and closed the side window leaving Simon and Yves to themselves and concentrated on take-off procedures. Once ready, he turned to Simon who was adjusting the seatbelt.

"I've had a message that we've got another passenger to pick up along the way, so we'll need to divert to Arras. I didn't want to tell you that in front of them as I was told to be discreet. You ready?" Rutherford shouted that he was as Mallow pushed on a rod that came out of the dashboard, and immediately the plane started to move.

Yves and Simon waited until the plane took off before getting back in the car. As they did so, two characters dressed in their distinctive suits and hats appeared from the end of the line of hangars.

"Merde! Our Bosch now know where your friend is."

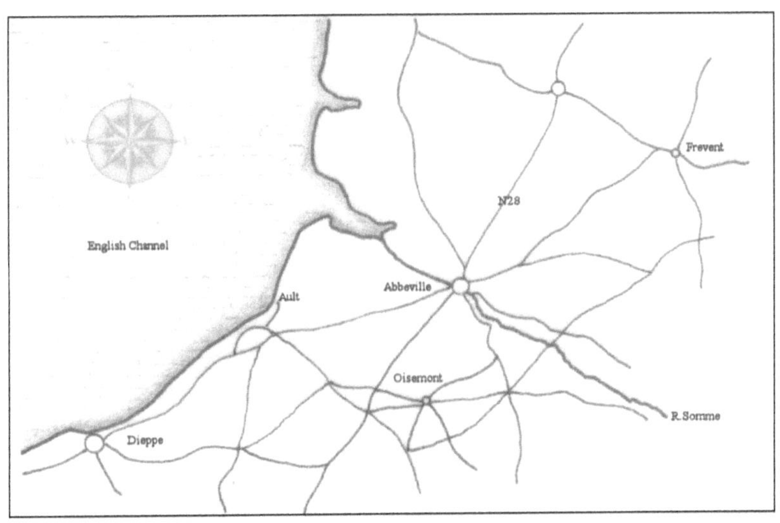

English Channel
Ault
Abbeville
N28
Frevent
Oisemont
Dieppe
R.Somme

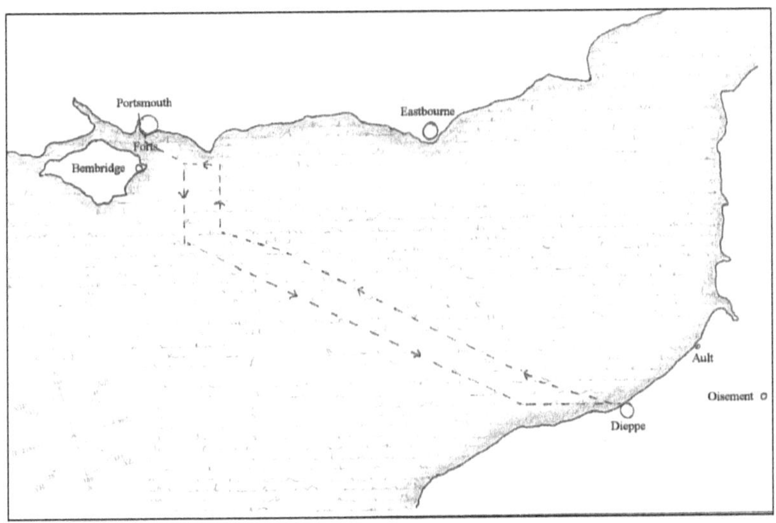

Portsmouth
Eastbourne
Ports.
Bembridge
Ault
Oisement
Dieppe

Chapter 2
The First Airfield

France – May 1940

Destroying an airfield in double-quick time was proving more awkward than he imagined. Second Lieutenant Bernard Stock wished the order had come a few hours earlier, or even later when he could have carried out his destruction under the cover of darkness, but now there were several hours of broad daylight left and the advancing Germans were not going to provide him with that respite.

'The Royal Air Force. Where's the RA bloody F just when you need them?' he thought to himself as he sensibly cowered behind a square pile of undistributed sandbags that protected him from the flying sheets of corrugated iron that had until just a moment ago been one of the hangars. 'If I wait here long enough the bloody Luftwaffe will do the job for me.' He stuck his fingers in his ears as a bomb exploded right next to Hangar B and distributed most of what he had recently been constructing, mainly in his direction. He involuntarily shut his eyes tight and waited for the debris to settle before gingerly leaning over to look around the side of his protective barrier. 'Only Hangar D left, and I expect they'll be back for that soon.'

He had heard the distinctive whine of the Stuka dive bombers before he saw the three of them diving from high up in formation from the southeast and had just enough time to fling himself behind the several tons of sandbags before the whistling bombs headed in his direction. Three Stukas. Four hangars… 'They'll be back for the last one,' he thought as he sat with his back resting against the soft sandy canvas and considered exactly what to do next when the wind wafted the faint drone of engines in his direction. It was impossible to tell where the buggers had gone but he scanned the sky away from the sun as it was pretty pointless looking towards it. Besides which, the expanding clouds of black smoke left him with little choice as to what he could actually see. This time they came in at low level from the west and, just in time, he scuttled round the side of his sandy shelter away from the exploding ground as machine gun shells spumed the earth only yards away. He huddled against his wall as close as he could. From under his armpit he watched a line of holes appear and tear up a line of wooden latrines. His wooden latrines. Bastards. Off to his left, he was vaguely aware that one of the other Stukas had successfully targeted one of the NAAFI stores and had left it in a similarly splintered condition as his latrines. He quickly discarded the thought of wishing he had a machine gun as he realised that the third Stuka had delayed its approach. He was in clear sight of it, but he had no time to duck behind the third side of the piled bags. Once again the ground erupted around him but this time he felt sand dribbling down his neck. 'Bloody Hell… that was close.' He felt a dampness spreading across his left leg. Wiping the sand away from his eyes, he studied his legs first of all, then his arms, and finally his body to see if any of it had become detached. He returned his gaze to his leg expecting to see a red stain of blood on his uniform, but, no, it was just wet. He reached out and retrieved some of the dampness with his finger and sniffed it. No, he hadn't wet himself; it was just water.

Very gingerly he looked up and around to locate his enemy. He could hear them and concluded they were somewhere to the north on the other side of the big sandy barrier that he now considered a life-saver. He realised his leg was becoming wetter and looked down to see an expanding rivulet of water heading in his direction. 'Must have got the water tower.' He focused on the nearby matchwood framework of what was formerly a functional utility but was now a useless grounded water tank with holes in it. The droning engines brought his attention back to self-preservation, but the three vultures had ceased their overhead circling and were leaving in the direction from where they had come.

Standing up, he automatically dusted himself down for a few seconds before realising that it was a pretty pointless exercise as swirling black flakes of ash were still airborne and settling on him. He looked over towards one of the empty billets that had not been touched except for their windows being blow inwards. That was where he had last seen Corporal Day heading when the Stukas had started their dive, and he felt a wave of relief as the large man appeared and waved at him to signal that he still had all his limbs. They met under the arched entrance to Hangar D as this was free from the acrid smoke that drifted in the other direction and, besides which, it also housed the last of the remaining transport: a pair of 500cc BSA M20 motorcycles.

"We had better get these moved sharpish before we lose these as well. The hedge behind here ought to do for the moment."

"Yes, sir."

"And let's put some extra fuel in the panniers."

Stock and Day fitted a two gallon can into each of the saddles that straddled the rear wheels and reluctantly he removed a bundle of black moleskins from one. Only last week, one of the pilots had berated him again about the number of molehills on the grass runway. "If I get a wheel stuck in one of those, I won't be able to take off and the CO's going to go berserk. Sort it out, will you."

He had tried pouring petrol down the holes and firing them, but this had had the opposite effect as the moles had simply made more hills trying to escape their singed burrows. He had asked one of the sergeants if he knew of anyone who knew how to deal with moles. Privates Aubrey and Strawberry had duly reported to him five minutes later and declared they could rid the airfield of all the moles in one night but on the one condition that nobody, including Stock, could see how they would do it. Stock had been sceptical, suspecting they just wanted a night off to meet local girls, and prepared himself to explain to the major the next morning why he had given such a free hand. When he rose the next morning he had berated himself for being taken in by such a stupid claim and strode out to find the two culprits who would be the cause of a dressing down by the major. In a foul mood, he had slammed the door shut behind him and taken two paces towards their hut before stopping still. They were standing to attention a few feet away with a pile of dead moles between them, hundreds of them. He had been speechless, and his gaping mouth brought smiles to the two chaps. They refused to tell him how they had done it, and to his dying day, he never found out.

They rode the BSAs over to the verdant hedge that would hopefully camouflage their presence from above. "Now, how about the rest of it?"

They both stood and surveyed what remained of the airfield. Apart from the crackling of burning timbers and the background roar of burning oil, it was completely silent, eerie and unsettling, when by comparison just a few hours before it had been a hive of activity. Now they felt as though they were alone in the world, abandoned and left to fend for themselves, but they still had a duty to perform and, ironically, the three Stukas had helped them do just that.

Stock's gaze focused on the large neatly stacked pile of forty-gallon fuel drums half a mile away that benefitted from the shade of the giant elm trees. Firing the excess fuel would be his last task before he finished demolishing what remained of the airfield just east of the sleepy town of Frévent. In the meantime, he and his corporal would have to make sure that there was nothing of any use left behind that could help the Germans.

"You go and sort out the last NAAFI store and Hangar D and I'll fire the billets and check the Messes. You know what to do, don't you?"

"Oh, yes, sir." Corporal Day beamed from ear to ear with the prospect of blowing up an entire hangar. It would simply be a matter of opening the cock on the almost empty fuel bowser and making sure that it set light to the half-built structure. They had not had the luxury of building the frame out of steel beams and had had to use local timber instead and its demolition was something they had been discussing when they had been interrupted by the three Stukas. He was also looking forward to being given free run in the NAAFI stores before he set light to it and would fill his pockets with as many cigarettes and other useful items as possible. He could sell them on later.

"Be quick about it! Oh, and shout before you put a match to it. I do not fancy being clobbered by flying sheets of corrugated iron again." As Stock walked towards the Officers' Mess, Day trotted in the direction of the wooden NAAFI store. Stock knew Day would take advantage of raiding the stores, but he didn't mind. He was a good fellow and, anyway, there was not much he would be able to carry in any case.

Stock mounted the two steps and stepped through the open door into the Officers' Mess. Despite his eyes smarting from the wafting oily smoke outside, he could see that everything was where it should be, except it was covered with shredded curtains and broken glass. He looked down to confirm that the briefcase he had left just inside the door earlier was still there and mournfully walked a few paces towards the bar counter that seemed to have fared better than its surroundings. After brushing away some of the debris, he instinctively rested one elbow on its top and allowed himself a moment of reflection; he felt that after what he had just been through, it was the least he deserved. 'God, but I could do with a drink right now,' he thought as he scanned the empty shelves which had, no doubt, been cleared by Steward Allan, partially for his own benefit. He casually leaned over to the hidden cupboard that normally housed the paraphernalia that goes with a bar and hoped that Allan had left behind something to drink in his secreted store. His eyes lit up when he spied a miniature Jonny Walker Red Label resting on a pad of chitty notes and retrieved both items. He read the note first. 'Knew you'd find it. Good luck, sir – see you in Blighty.' Stock laughed out loud, unscrewed the top and emptied the nectar into his mouth in one. He swilled it for a moment, savouring its peaty flavour before letting it gently descend down his throat. 'God bless you, Allan.' The precious liquid tingled its way down his gullet and proceeded to warm his belly as he rested both elbows on the counter and clasped the tiny bottle in both hands. 'Just what the doctor ordered.' The young Allan had been about to embark on a career in the medical profession when he had been conscripted and this had earned him the nickname of 'The Doctor.' In the Mess he often helped his customers concoct unusual mixtures of spirits and tonics. On one occasion…

Whoooooommp. The external noise brought Stock back to his senses, and he twisted round and crouched at the same time in case it wasn't Corporal Day's doing. 'Enough of this,' he thought as he reached into the same cupboard for a box of matches and snatched up a small heap of out-of-date newspapers by his feet. He scrumpled up a few sheets and put a match to them under one of the chairs in the far corner before repeating the exercise nearer the door. By the time he reached it, acrid smoke accompanied the growing flames that only an extinguisher could put out. On his way out, he kicked a smouldering cushion so that the air could fan the flames, picked up his briefcase and strode out of the mess, clutching the newspapers.

Now en route to the nearest billet, he glanced over and saw that Day had fired the NAAFI hut which had bright flames reaching haphazardly out of the broken windows and didn't give it a further thought as he eyed up the wind direction to ascertain which billet to set light to first. The nearest would mean he wouldn't be blinded by smoke from the others, and he repeated his arsonist pursuit to the next four buildings. He also considered the 'quad' of four large field tents a little further on, but he soon put these out of his mind as hot media from the other huts floated in their direction and indeed one of them was already smouldering.

A shout from Day. He looked to his right and through the patchy smoke saw the big man about a hundred yards away gesticulating with what looked like a blow torch in one hand and a towel in the other. Stock gave him the thumbs up and headed for the relative safety of the hedge behind him in anticipation of another explosion. He had just reached it when he stopped, turned and thought for a moment. 'Now what would Day want with a blow torch when he had matches in his pocket?' He wiped the tearful grime from his eyes and saw Day sprinting towards him for all he was worth; he never knew he could run so fast.

"Best get behind this hedge, sir….just in case." And he darted through a small gap. Stock followed.

Day was bent over, resting his hands on his knees, trying to get his breath back. Stock waited until his heaving body recovered enough while looking through the hedge at Hangar D, waiting for something to happen. "I'm intrigued, Corporal. Was that a blow torch I saw you holding up?"

Day stood up and beamed back at his officer. "Thought I'd make a proper job if it, sir." His heaving chest was returning to normal, and he placed his hands on his hips. "You see, with all that petrol it wouldn't give me much time to get away before it exploded so I looked around and found a couple of barrels of creosote." He gave a mighty sigh indicating that he was back to normal now, stood fully upright and joined Stock peering through the hedge.

Stock waited for more as it still didn't answer why the blowtorch and Day saw the quizzical look on his face. "I put the barrels under the bowser and pierced them with a screwdriver, then left the blowtorch warming them up nicely. The trouble was that that torch is a bit broken, and the handle gets hot very quickly but it oughtn't to be long now." He returned to peering through the hedge; as did Stock. They waited… and waited.

"There wasn't all that much petrol in the bowser which is why I used the creosote, and it ought to have caught by now. It ought to be flooding all over the ground. Do you want me to go and have a look?" Day volunteered.

Stock considered for a moment. "No, I'll do it. You wait here. Let's give it another minute though." He looked down at his watch, not really relishing the prospect of going anywhere near that hangar.

One minute later Stock took a step sideways to go through the hedge when they both felt rather than heard the explosion that ripped apart Hangar D. They instinctively ducked and looked away, waiting for an abatement before returning to their spy holes in the hedge.

Corporal Day was once again beaming from ear to ear, relieved that his scheme had worked and that his officer would not need to doubt his abilities anymore. "Told you it would work, sir.... proper job." They had both gone back through the hedge and stood surveying the blazing wreckage of ex-Hangar D.

Stock nodded in approval "Like you say, Corporal, proper job. Well done. Now, I suppose we ought to attend to that fuel dump." He nodded towards the trees in the distance where there was considerably more fuel, so much of it that he was now worried how they would fire it while managing to still stay alive. "How much petrol do you reckon there is there?"

Day returned his look and then realised why he was being asked that question. "Aaah… well, there's got to be about two hundred barrels. No, wait a minute, I overheard the Major cussing the transport mob when they delivered another two hundred the other day. Seems someone doubled up on the order so there's probably nearer four hundred barrels. I think they were due to be delivered to the Arras airfield."

Stock did a mental calculation of four hundred times forty. That made sixteen thousand gallons of petrol. Oh, well, that would go with some bang. "Let's get the motorcycles and go over there. Where did you leave our kit?"

"I put yours and mine together in the guard hut by the main entrance as I thought we would be leaving that way. Do you want me to get them?"

"No, leave them there. We'll have to get onto that road anyway."

As they strode over to where they had left the BSA's, Stock looked at their handiwork that had taken less time than previously thought due to the intervention of the Luftwaffe. He inwardly chuckled. He'd spent five weeks constructing and expanding this airfield's buildings and it had taken less than five hours to destroy them. He hoped this was not going to be an augury of the rest of his military career.

On Stock's indication, they dismounted the BSA's behind the edge of the wood a sensible distance from the nearest fuel drum. Stock was appalled. From this aspect of the airfield, billowing black smoke was now drifting almost vertically and would be seen for miles. No, tens of miles in this clear air, and it surely must attract some attention. Without the aid of his binoculars, he gazed closely along the far perimeter and thought he saw the outline of a few people, hopefully from the local village, and wondered if it was anybody he knew.

Frévent lay in the shadow of a decent escarpment which ran north-west to south- east making it an ideal location for any plane taking off into the wind that prevailed from the south-west. It wasn't large enough to be called a town and Stock had only driven through it once while on a recce and it had appeared like most of the other villages he had gone through; quiet. Testament to its main industry of crops were the miles and miles of tended fields that surrounded the area, and Stock had presumed that this is where their daily supply of fresh bread had come from.

On his recce, he had stopped near the town centre as he was not certain which road led him to where he had wanted to go. An ageing but agile woman had appeared from a doorway and, while asking her for directions in his very poor French with the help of a map had been given, he had noticed she was carrying a deep wicker basket. Lifting the chequered cloth, he saw and smelt the cheeses at the same time. Such a wonderful mouth-watering aroma was irresistible, and he offered to buy one of them with the few francs he had. Instead, she had led him back through the doorway. Stock had to duck down a little as they passed through a passage to the rear of the building which opened into a semi-enclosed courtyard where the strong smell of cheese overpowered almost everything else. There were two teenagers working at a long table on one side while opposite Stock could feel the presence of livestock through another open doorway. The smoothed cobblestones beneath him sloped down to an open gully nearer the far side, and he saw the whey dribbling down through it from the stone press, just off to one side. He had realised he had stumbled across the village cheesemaker. He loved cheese. He had left there some two hours later after being introduced to other members of the family while being virtually force-fed wine and cheeses. He was happily clutching two small cakes of soft cheese, one which he had later used to curry favour with the airfield commander. A few days later, one of the teenage boys had cycled up to the airfield with a pannier-full of the same cheese and sold it to the NAFFI sergeant. Second Lieutenant Stock's standing was on the up as the lad's visits became more frequent.

Perhaps it was a slight pick-up in the breeze, or it may have been the sound of another can of creosote catching fire, but it brought Stock's attention back to the task in hand. And then he heard it again. That last noise had not come from Hangar D but much further away. It was difficult to tell from which direction. It was faint, the kind of noise that reverberated off the distance. A bit like thunder.

Stock well knew that he could not allow themselves to be anywhere near by when the first fuel drum exploded. He'd learned that lesson years ago on his family farm when he had accidently punctured a small canister of petrol with a pick-axe and the sparks had immediately ignited the volatile vapour and singed his hair. This lot was more likely to cremate them both.

Day stood to one side as Stock drew his service Webley revolver and took aim.

"Ready?" Day had his fingers in his ears and didn't hear him.

Stock steadied his arm, held his breath and pulled the trigger. This would be the first time he had actually fired his revolver 'in anger' but he remembered his training and elevated the gun a little higher than he had done so before. They both saw the .38 lead slug land in the grass about a hundred feet short of the nearest barrel.

"I think you're going to have to get closer, sir." Day was stating the obvious but also in the hope that he wouldn't have to get closer himself.

Stock gave him a baleful look, before pacing out the requisite distance that would bring him into range and stopped just short. This time he raised his arm to what he considered about forty-five degrees and fired. A metallic clang proclaimed his accuracy, and he crouched down facing the opposite direction, expecting a great roar of an explosion. Nothing happened.

He gently stood up and surveyed the peaceful scene, deciding he must get closer still. The number thirty came into his head, maybe because he had recently celebrated his thirtieth birthday, so he paced out thirty steps nearer the petroleum monster that seemed to be defying him. He was now less than a hundred yards away. Once again he took aim and fired, repeating his cowering pose in anticipation as another clang rang out. Nothing happened.

What had started out as being a simple job in his own mind had now turned into quite a dilemma. There had never been anything in his field manual about blowing up fuel dumps. He certainly didn't want to get much closer, but he had to, and he paced off another fifteen steps. This time he took particular aim at one of the nearest drums on the upper tier. He had made up his mind that, whatever the outcome, he would stand his ground and watch the bullet as it entered the drum before diving for the ground. He looked round at Day as if to say goodbye before taking a deep breath and firing.

He saw the slug tearing into the centre of the drum and watched as golden liquid spouted from the hole, like a man relieving himself badly. Still no explosion.

He felt he was being toyed with by some greater power and decided he was going to have to give this some more thought, as he holstered his revolver. Corporal Day came over to him of his own accord. "That's the weirdest thing I've ever seen. It ought to have gone up by now. Perhaps it's not petrol at all?"

Stock was beginning to think the same thing but there was one certain way to tell. "Come on, we'll go and have a look."

They closed on the pile of drums with trepidation, half expecting them to blow up in their faces, but they didn't, they just sat there like a lump. They were within a few feet when Stock smelt the fumes and he looked over his shoulder at Day to make sure he wasn't smoking. Definitely petrol. He could see now that his previous shots had just dented the metal containers but his last had indeed penetrated and it now spouted petrol into its own puddle on the ground, but there was no sign of anything approaching an explosion anywhere. Stock played his foot over the puddling petrol trying to understand what had gone wrong but then it dawned on him like a rebuke from the sergeant major, that his firing his revolver at the drums was never going to produce a spark. His bullets were made of lead, not the new full metal jacket that was now becoming more commonplace, and it was never going to be possible, however many times he shot at the drums, for them to ignite the fumes. They were just too soft and slow to make a spark.

He turned to Day. "Where's your 303?" He was referring to the standard issue Lee Enfield rifle issued to all non-commissioned soldiers. "That's got the new ammunition hasn't it."

Day gulped. "It's over by the guard hut, sir." They both looked in that direction, over half a mile away. "And I've only got one magazine." He saw the look of distaste in Stock's eyes and added, "I was ordered to travel as light as possible, sir, and I didn't think we'd need it all the way over here." His mitigating bleat did little to calm Stock's now rising anger at the situation. He was about to send Day over to retrieve his rifle when he heard a familiar boom in the distance, the same as he had heard before only this time closer. Whether or not it was the wind, Stock recognised it as artillery fire, and it was coming closer. Time was running out.

Stock abruptly turned back towards the drums and tapped his boot in the deepening puddle. What to do, what to do? He ceased his tapping and looked down. Of course! The sergeant major was shouting in his ear again, berating him for not thinking quicker and he looked around at the lay of the land. Yes. This would work. But… He felt in his pocket and mercifully found the box of matches he had borrowed from the Mess. Yes…

He spun round on Day. "Quick. Give me a hand with this drum. We'll roll it down the slope here towards the end of the runway and fire it all from there."

Forty-gallon drums are not light, even just to tip over onto their side, but they managed to ease it over and let it fall onto the ground. Stock then realised another problem confronted them. By rolling it away to a safe distance with just one hole in the side would mean that there would be patches of petrol on the grass, not a continuous trail. He drew his revolver again, aimed at one of the drums on the upper tier so that it would leave a decent amount of vapour in the air around the dump to ignite, then walked a few feet to one end of their drum.

"Stand back!" At almost point-blank range he shot another hole into one end. The light amber liquid spumed now that there was no vacuum to restrain its flow. "Come on. Let's get it rolling. Quickly, but not too quickly. That way, downhill."

On a warm summer's day like today, the fuel would evaporate in no time, but he had to judge that against the amount needed on the trail to ensure a continuous flame. He looked over his shoulder to see how far they had come. Just another few feet ought to do it, he thought, just as the hole in the end glugged for the first time. But he had another problem because now there were two sources of the highly inflammable liquid he would have to deal with. They stopped rolling far too soon as far as Day was concerned.

"Run! Back to the BSAs!" Stock ordered Day as he felt into his pocket for the box of matches and trotted several yards back up the invisible trail they had just made. The air was becoming thicker with petrol vapour, and he knew he had to act immediately before he became embroiled in the impeding inferno. With the briefest of glances to his right to check that Day was doing as he was told, he struck a match and bent down to the grass while it was still flaring. Still nothing.

The match was having more success in setting fire to the grass than he was in trying to ignite a far more inflammable substance. 'Must have missed the trail,' he thought, and struck another match while lining himself up more accurately between the dump and their primed drum before crouching down again. Still nothing, as the match fizzled out. He was starting to get seriously worried that this task was not a simple as it first appeared. He looked down into the box at the dwindling supply of matches and was just drawing out one of the last few when he heard a 'Whooooomp' at his feet. He looked down and was horrified to see that he had actually succeeded in lighting the trail as it flamed black oily smoke in opposite directions at the same time. It took him all of one second to react and he turned to sprint in the same direction as Day.

He managed half-a-dozen strides before he heard the nearer primed drum explode first over his right shoulder, but he kept on running without looking back, knowing that the monster behind his left shoulder would become all too apparent very quickly. He was still a very fit man at the age of thirty and it was known in his local rugby club that he could sprint the hundred yards in under thirteen seconds, but he wasn't timing himself now nor counting paces. He just knew he had to get away as far as he could. He did however have time to pray to himself that this would work as he saw Corporal Day up ahead turn and run towards the BSAs. His prayers were answered all too soon. Over his left shoulder he heard the first barrel on the top tier explode followed by louder staccatos. Still, he didn't look back. He never saw it coming, but the air around him seemed demonised as he felt a thump on his back, and he was falling headfirst into the ground. As he lay there, he briefly compared his grounded state to that of being fully tackled by the opposition's No.8,, and then sat on. His ears hurt from the noise, his head and chest hurt from the impact with the hard ground, his back hurt from the whack he had received, his eyes felt as though they were trying to escape from their sockets and his left thumb hurt for some other reason he could not comprehend at the moment. He covered his head with his hands and lay as still as he could, feeling the intense heat wax and wane over him as individual or groups of drums released their satanic energy.

How long he lay there he couldn't tell, but later, Corporal Day had told him that one flaming barrel had cannoned itself right over him and that had he been standing up at the time so it wouldn't have been for long. He opened his eyes and for several seconds gasped for the breath that had been knocked out of him, removed his hand from his head, and slowly rolled over onto his right side to get a better view of the fuel dump. Sitting up to get a better view he was amazed. Fortunately, the slight breeze was taking the smoke off to his left, leaving him with a clear view of the shattered trees. Like a child's balsa wood model aeroplane left on the floor and trodden on by a giant, the complete corner of the wood had disintegrated leaving behind splintered stumps, surrounded by flaming trunks and branches. A loud bang on the far side out of his sightline announced that the still flaming wreckage had found another laden drum, and he briefly saw its flaming trajectory disappear in the other direction.

'I've done it, I've actually done it,' he thought to himself. 'Perhaps I can now put that in the manual.' Stock grinned but stopped immediately as it hurt his ears. He hadn't heard him approach, but Day now stood in front of him, offering his hand out to help him up. He gladly took the offer.

"Well done, sir." A grinning Day bent over and retrieved Stock's cap from some feet away. "That went with a bang. Proper job, sir." They both flinched as the flames found another full victim, again on the far side.

Day was looking at Stock and craned his head to see better. "Are you alright, sir? I can see blood on your cheek."

Day's voice to Stock was slightly muffled but he put his hand up to his cheek and felt the familiar sticky wetness of blood.

"Looks like it's coming from your ear, sir." He gathered a handkerchief from his pocket and watched Stock wipe the blood away from his cheek. Stock didn't realise he was looking down at his own thumb that was sticking out at an odd angle. In a dazed state, it took him a while to understand that he had dislocated it, probably when he had been blown to the ground, but he was not worried. It had happened to several of his digits when playing rugby and the solution was simple. Day stopped staring and prudently he didn't say anything, recognising that his officer was still a bit stunned.

"Come on, sir. Time to get back to the bikes." But there was no movement from Stock who just stood and stared at his misplaced digit. It took just a gentle touch on his elbow from Day before Stock returned to reality. He suddenly grasped his thumb in his right hand and forced it back into position.

Stock held his left hand up and wiggled his replaced thumb a little. "Thank you, Corporal. Yes, let's go!"

It wasn't until they reached the BSAs did Stock turn back for a final look and began to think, like Corporal Day, 'a proper job.' In truth, it was a real mess. What had once been a peaceful country scene that any painter might have been proud to study was now a complete shambles. Then again, that same painter might have wanted to study such an unusual sight. Stock gazed up at the billowing smoke caused by the efforts of the Luftwaffe and their own contributions and concluded that they really didn't want to be there for much longer. If the German army was advancing as quickly as they had been told, they were bound to investigate sooner rather than later.

They kick-started their BSAs, cycled around those smoky clouds that had not managed to gain any altitude, and headed for the main gate to collect their packs. About halfway across the airfield, Stock thought he saw the outline of a man darting behind the guard hut. Probably one of the locals the thought, and then eased off the throttle as he realised that he hadn't reloaded his revolver and he couldn't remember if he had fired five or six shots. Come to that, his spare ammunition was with his kit. Better not tell that to Corporal Day.

Dismounting, Stock unholstered his Webley and made sure it was pointing at the ground so that whoever it was would not be able to see that there were no bullets in the chambers; the threat alone ought to be sufficient. "Go and get your rifle. I'll cover you."

Day nearly took the first step automatically before he too realised that Stock had not reloaded. He paused, then carried on to the hut a few paces away. Even before he reappeared with his rifle in the doorway, Stock had started to circle round to see if there was really anyone behind the hut, but it wasn't until he was almost parallel with the back of it did he see a leather shoe protruding. Whoever it was had his back tight against the wall of the wooden hut and was trying not to be visible.

"Come out."

Almost immediately a suited man holding a briefcase emerged.

"Thank God you're English." He all but collapsed and sat with his arms resting on his knees and his back against the hut. His heavy breathing and closed eyes under his brimmed hat gave the impression that he was recovering from heavy exercise, which is exactly what he had been doing.

On hearing the educated English voice, Stock relaxed a bit but still kept his revolver out. "Who are you and what are you doing here?" Day had appeared and was pointing his rifle at the man from behind.

Stock waited for the man to take a few more deep breaths before opening his eyes and meeting Stock's stare.

Still sitting down, he started to explain, "My name's Rutherford …… I've spent the last three days keeping out of the clutches of the Germans…..and it's very important that I get back to England sharpish." He paused to take a last deep breath and stood up. He was about the same average height as Stock, maybe a bit older but with an unshaven face that portrayed a weariness. Dried rivulets of sweat and grime emerged from under the brim of his hat, one overlaid with a new bead that flowed freely down his left cheek. Rutherford removed his hat, revealing a receding dark brown hairline.

"It's a long story and I haven't got time to tell you it all now, but the Germans are advancing fast. About half-an-hour ago, I was down in that village and had to pinch a bike to keep ahead of them. I can tell you, that's a bloody long hill when you've got to cycle up it and I'm not as fit as I used to be. I didn't have much choice really as this was pretty much the only road they haven't blocked off. It's not going to take them long to figure out I'm no longer in the village and, when they do, I think it highly likely they'll head in this direction, thanks to your wonderful pyrotechnic display." His head motioned to where the fuel dump had previously been. "Now, is there any chance you can get me some transport?" He looked over Stock's shoulder to see what there was available.

Stock put his revolver away, indicated that Day could stand down, and started to assess the man in front of him. It was clear that this was no ordinary Englishman; his superior attitude, Oxford accent, clarity of diction all added up to someone who was used to dealing with military types, although he had not announced his rank. Stock always liked to know the man next to him; something his father had impressed upon him: 'It's who you know that gets you further.'

He considered the request and saw the funny side of it. "Help yourself to the fleet of trucks over there. I think we can squeeze him in, can't we, Corporal?"

Day was nonplussed and just stood there, but Rutherford fell for it by looking down the hedgerow for all of three seconds before realising he had been had. He smiled so that Stock could see and took in the reality, "Are you the last ones here?"

Stock didn't answer straight away. If this man was intelligent he would be able to answer that for himself and deduce that they were about to leave. It also wouldn't take him long to realise that

Stock was not going to concede anything until he had been given an explanation.

The ploy worked.

"Look," said Rutherford taking a pace nearer Stock, "I'm not permitted to tell you why, but I really must return to England straight away and certainly before the Germans get hold of what's in this case, but I need your help to do that. What I can tell you for certain is that they are not far away and will be here in a matter of minutes. Can you help? Please?"

Stock had half expected this condescending pitch, but he had already made his mind up. "Ever been on a bike before?" he responded with a look that said he already knew the answer.

Rutherford felt a little 'put-down' by Stock's retort and glanced at the pair of BSAs a few yards away, "I'm sure I can manage to hang on to you." He decided not to emphasis the 'You' part of it as this might well upset the second lieutenant in front of him and he didn't want to do that. Not yet, and then maybe not at all.

But Stock wasn't finished with him yet. "What's so important about the case?" It wasn't large but it wouldn't fit into one of the panniers now that they had extra fuel in them. Stock and Day had previously loaded the bikes with some of their own kit which was securely roped down and this would need to be rearranged to take a passenger with a case.

"I'll tell you what, you get us out of here, ten miles away from the Germans and I'll tell you more. It won't be much but suffice to say that it's a military matter and no, I am not a smuggler."

"Fair enough. Corporal Day.....my map please." Day returned from the hut a few seconds later clutching the map case Stock had been given by the airfield's commander that morning. "We'll take this road up to Saint-Pol and keep heading north until we reach the Calais road, we can then turn right to Dunkirk. Ought to take us the best part of the day."

"You can't go there!" Rutherford's exclamation was emphatic.

"Why not?"

"You physically cannot get to Dunkirk. In fact, you won't be able to get past the Calais road. The Germans have almost surrounded it. I should know as I've just come from that direction."

Perhaps this man might not be a hindrance after all, Stock mused. "Show me." Day crowded round as Stock shared the map in Rutherford's direction.

"Just here," he pointed just north of Arras about sixty miles to the east. "They broke through our lines. I was waiting for an aircraft to take me back to England, but we didn't get far, and I was almost trapped. Like you, I tried to reach Dunkirk, but the Calais road was impassable. Convoy after convoy of Germans and they weren't loitering and that was two days ago. By now, I expect they'll have reached Calais."

Rutherford let Stock take in the obvious. At least, it was obvious to him, and he hoped Stock would come to the same conclusion without any more prompting. "I'm trying to reach Dieppe as I know the Germans haven't got that far yet and there's bound to be ships sailing back to England from there."

Stock's orders had been to make for Dunkirk where an evacuation was taking place, but only after he had completed wrecking the airfield. An evacuation from one port or another was neither here nor there to him, but he was reluctant to deviate from his orders. There was the muster station he had been told to report to, and probably a designated ship at Dunkirk. If he and Day were not there, he would be in trouble.

"I'm sorry but we have been ordered to Dunkirk."

"Please believe me when I tell you, you will never make it."

"We shall see, but that's where we've been ordered to and that's where we're going. Corporal Day, get ready to leave." Stock's decision was clearly final.

But Rutherford wasn't giving up. "Look, I'll tell you what. You see this road here that runs parallel to the Calais road? I think it's the old road. Get onto that and you can see for yourself."

Stock was becoming suspicious of this man. How did this chap know about the roads, where the Germans were, what they were doing, where the ships were? All these things were unknown to him, yet a complete stranger, a civilian stranger at that, had suddenly appeared and claimed to know everything. He had given him the benefit of the doubt before but now was feeling inclined just to leave him here, although he knew he couldn't.

"We'll take you as far as you want to go. You can get off at any time. OK?"

"OK. But you really will see what I'm talking about when we get nearer."

Chapter 3
The Fourth Child

Bernard Stock was born shortly before King Edward VII passed away in 1910 and grew up on the extensive Norfolk farming land which had been in his family for generations. With his parents and aunt and three other siblings they shared the large manor house that dated back to the early 1800's. With it came two cooks, a gardener, and Bill the maintenance man, who Bernard got on particularly well with. Several full-time 'hands' were helped by regular, if not vagrant wanderers, who appeared every harvest and were well-paid for their brief services.

He was far from the 'black sheep' of the family, but his determination to resolve any awkward problem in his own way, rather than the more traditional manner, set him not just aside, but aloof from his contemporaries. He spurned the old ways of farming in favour of what he considered more practical methods. He was forever making models or creating miniature dams in the numerous dykes and ditches that criss-crossed the estate, and even made himself handy by improving the design of one of the many water pumps that helped drain those ditches. However, his respect within the family took a definite downturn when trying to improve the shape of the harness that bound the massive draft horses to the ploughs that furrowed the wheat fields. The new shape of the brass shackle eventually caused Bessie, one of the lead-horses, to go lame from the shoulder, and his father, Charles, in an attempt to teach the young Bernard that he was responsible for his own actions, gave him the job of putting Bessie down. His brothers and sisters stood and watched as the tender, young Bernard was handed the heavy horse pistol. The horse's long suffering was finally put to a swift end, but not before the taunts of his siblings sunk deep into his soul, and fond memories of the great beast etched permanently into Bernard's mind.

His love of creation and the simple mechanics that made things work drew Bernard closer to the new machinery that was being made available to the farming community up and down the country. He saved his hard-earned pocket money to visit the local night school in Dereham and improve on his already good grasp of mechanics. This was where he made most of his life-long friends.

Although he was still growing as he reached his eighteenth birthday, he enjoyed being nearly six feet tall and being able to look over the heads of others. Much to his father's gratification, he worked hard on the estate from the age of seven, learning as much as he could from those around him and thoroughly enjoyed the company of the labourers. Their brusque language peculiar to that part of the world took some getting used to. At school he was taught the King's English but he adapted easily, depending upon whose company he was keeping at the time. It didn't matter to him if he was ditching, fencing, building, harvesting, ploughing, or anything else that needed to be done, he always put his back into it and earned the respect that went with it.

One summer's day during his thirteenth year, his father had irked his siblings by telling them that he would only be taking Bernard to the cattle market in Norwich; he was now old enough to learn about the art of buying and selling cattle at the auctions. He felt a little out of place, not knowing anybody and needing to look up at strange faces, but his father was in his element and was constantly shaking hands, introducing Bernard whenever he thought it appropriate. He led them over to the stock pens where the bulls were held temporarily prior to the auctions. Finding a quiet corner en route, he took Bernard to one side, "It's quite an art selecting the right bull and you can't always tell from just looking at the animal how strong it is, and don't go believing some of these rogues who will tell you exactly what you want to hear, once they find out what you are after. They won't go as far as forging certificates but I haven't come across a bull yet that wasn't related to a grand champion somewhere down the line."

He looked around to make sure they weren't being observed, put his right forefinger and thumb into his waistcoat pocket and withdrew a neatly folded cloth that surrounded a small brown phial. "This is one of our family secrets so don't go telling anyone else, not even your siblings. My father taught me, and I expect his father taught him so let's keep it that way. It's akin to smelling salts to cattle. Once we get back home I'll show you what's in it, but it doesn't smell so bad to us humans. Depending upon how the bull reacts to it will tell you a lot about the animal. You need to waft the cloth fairly close to its nose. If it just stands there morosely and moves slowly away, this tells you that it has mucus up its nostrils and probably has something wrong with its lungs, but if it rears away and bellows then it's a healthy animal.

He unscrewed the cap and let three drops fall onto the cloth before screwing the lid back on. Bernard immediately caught the aroma of something similar to chives or perhaps cloves; he couldn't tell which.

"Now, come with me and learn."

They walked casually over to the first pen where a large black and white bull stood with its snout not too far from the metal railings. With a last look around, his father leaned forward, rested both forearms on the upper rail and shook the cloth with one hand. "If anyone asks, it's your handkerchief. You can even wipe your nose with it if you must, but don't breathe in."

The animal saw them approach, but Bernard wasn't sure if it blinked in acknowledgement or if it was because of the fly that landed on its eyeball. His father unscrewed his hand and flapped the cloth, but there was no reaction. "You can see by the way it stands with its legs more under it, that it is trying to support itself and take the pressure of its front leg muscles. I think we'll give this one a miss. We don't want a Friesian anyway, we're after a Hereford. Look, over there."

They walked across the open alleyway to a much larger animal whose belly hung ponderously close to the ground. "Now, this is more like it. Here, you have a go, but hide that cloth quickly."

Bernard found the cloth being pushed surreptitiously into his left hand and repeated his father's previous operation close to its ringed nose, less than three feet away. A booming roar emanated from somewhere within the beast as it smartly backed away and reversed itself into the railings, which shook and rattled under the impact. Faces turned their way to see what all the rumpus was about but, by then, they were both standing a few feet away as if nothing had happened.

"Well done, my boy. He'll do nicely, I think."

They looked into each other's eyes. For the first time in his life, Bernard felt a real affinity between them.

He kept himself fit at all times, by joining the local rugby team during the winters and alternated between the tennis and cricket clubs during the summers, always striving to be better than the man next to him, whether a competitor or not. On his last day at school, his father summoned him to his study after tea.

"Well, my boy, you have just finished your schooling. You can either join us here on the estate or go into the army. Let me know in the morning."

His father had been an officer in the 17th Lancers and had seen action in South Africa during the first Boer war in 1881, and naturally expected Bernard to follow in his footsteps. Being a practical man, Charles recognised Bernard's natural aptitude for all things mechanical and, after two years, eventually acceded to Bernard's request to join the Royal Engineers, sponsoring his application to enlist as a second lieutenant.

Unmarried at the outbreak of the Second World War, the regiment became his world.

Chapter 4
Matilda

Stock led the way, glancing over his shoulder as they exited the gate and spotted a familiar bicycle discarded in the hedge. No more cheese for anybody for a while, he thought. Rutherford was his very uncomfortable pillion passenger, but Day on the other BSA was quite at home on the powerful machine and was exhilarated as he opened the throttle wide on the straight, yet narrow road. Stock had memorised the first few turnings they would have to make and wouldn't need to look down at his map case that was strapped to the fuel tank for quite a while. As they approached the junction of the D82 where they would have to turn right, the sergeant major shouted in his ear again. 'Frogs drive on the right – be there if you don't want to be flattened like one.' Stopping briefly to check the crossroads for non-existent traffic, he looked to his left. Now that they were some three miles from the airfield, he could see what Rutherford had meant by his pyrotechnical display. The dirty smoke was like a giant arrow in the clear blue sky pointing down to anybody who was looking for a landmark, and if there were Germans nearby, well, they could hardly miss it.

Corporal George Alfred Day was thoroughly enjoying himself. As a young boy brought up in the sprawling village of Over not far from the county town of Cambridge where agriculture kept the inhabitants employed, he had watched his uncle - who lived in one of the terraced estate cottages at the end of the row - lovingly restore his own father's Triumph model H motorcycle. After school, but only once his homework had been done, his mother would let him help Uncle Bert tinkering with the belt-driven 500cc machine.

"It's called a 'Trusty' because you can trust it. Never lets you down," his uncle had told him.

It seemed to take years to put back together and indeed it did, but on his eleventh birthday he watched Uncle Bert kick start it into life once again. As a treat, he had been hauled onto the bar above the fuel tank in front of his uncle and he thought that the thumping engine between his legs would explode as Bert fed some more fuel into it. He'd never been so fast in his life before. After the initial shock, he had looked down at the dial just in front of him to see they were going nearly twenty-five miles per hour. He had never owned his own motorcycle and never been on another, but ever since that day he had dreamed of it and now that dream had come true. He looked down at his own speedometer which hovered around the forty mark, and jiggled the BSA left and right on the open road, feeling it respond to him and him alone. One of the benefits of being conscripted into the Royal Engineers was that he got to drive trucks about, mainly after repairing them, and he revelled in the joy of working on anything mechanical. He more or less kept pace with Stock and Rutherford in front, occasionally dropping back a little so he could accelerate and enjoy the power as he neared them again.

The small town of Saint-Pol-sur-Ternoise was deserted; nobody anywhere. Stock took advantage of the empty streets and followed signs to Auchel on the D916, about another ten miles further on. That was where they were going to turn north-west and intersect with the parallel road Rutherford had mentioned.

Either side of them on the almost straight undulating roads were fields upon fields of ripening wheat. An occasional wooden shack, a granary here and there, a water tower at fairly regular intervals, buildings that looked like stables, irrigation ditches, a line of trees in the distance that never seemed to get any closer, but no signs of anybody else. Stock opened the throttle a little more to compensate for the slight hill and glanced down at his map knowing that they would soon reach the crossroads just before Auchel. Breasting the rise, he slowed down as he caught sight of the smudgy brown mist over the town a few miles away. He could see the crossroads in the gentle valley, but he could also see German trucks moving on the road they wanted to take. He stalled the BSA, kicked out the stand, dismounted, extracted his binoculars from the left-hand pannier and assumed the traditional pose when looking through binoculars.

Starting at the crossroads he saw that the road had been barricaded from their direction. Panning left, he counted the first four trucks, then a gap of about five hundred yards, then a convoy of nine trucks before the lead one disappeared out of sight round a wood. 'Damn, perhaps Rutherford was right.' Just then he heard the sound of artillery coming from somewhere beyond the crossroads, but he couldn't tell if it was 'ours or theirs.'

Taking the map from its pouch he considered their options. If the Germans were going north, there really was no point in trying to go that way too, as they would only stop when they reached the coast, and that would mean that they could not get through to Dunkirk. They could easily traverse the crossroads when the Germans had passed through but - assuming Rutherford was correct - they would most likely run into more of them. Besides which, Germany was that way, and it was the natural direction from where they would be attacking. South was not really an option as that would mean going back through Frévent. Stock made up his mind that they would follow Rutherford's plan to head for Dieppe. They would go west. But first they would need to find their way to Abbeville. Stock looked up at the sound of another big gun firing in the distance and saw Day and Rutherford standing a few yards away, looking at him.

"Dieppe it is.'

He didn't want to engage in conversation with Rutherford which would end up with him eating humble pie. "We'll go back to the last fork in the road and head for Abbeville on the D70." He handed the map to Rutherford. "I take it you can navigate so you'd better take this." He turned smartly and replaced the goggles over his eyes to indicate that Rutherford was going to read the map, whether or not he could navigate their way through the back lanes. Anyway, Stock had the sun to go by in case he couldn't, and it wasn't going to set for a few hours yet. He was just about to kick his machine into life when he heard the familiar drone of an aeroplane.

"Hold on a minute," he shouted at Day who had already started to turn around. The single drone quickly turned into several. Looking eastwards into the sky, saw a flight of twin-engined bombers heading towards the coast and not so high that they might not ignore them. "Let's wait until those buggers have moved on."

They came across very few vehicles and only a couple of locals over the next three hours as they traversed the same type of countryside that surrounded Frévent. Rutherford would tap him on the shoulder and point with one arm or another to indicate which turning Stock should take, occasionally stopping completely at a junction for a closer look at a steadier map. Twice they had to retrace their route, once when they came across a small river that wasn't on the map and another when Rutherford had taken the wrong turning at a complex crossroads. Stock was satisfied at their progress, yet it was becoming more and more difficult to drive directly into the setting sun. He was reluctant to stop until they reached Abbeville. 'Can't be much longer,' he thought as Rutherford indicated for him to stop again.

"Do you want to go through Abbeville or cross the river to the south?" Rutherford was leaning over with the map. "We're about here."

Stock saw that they had come a bit too far south, but he wasn't going to berate Rutherford there and then. "As far as I can tell, there's only three bridges over the Somme through the town but as we're over half-way there, why don't we use this bridge down here?" So far they had kept to the side roads, more out of necessity than choice as no main roads went in the direction they needed to take. They were now close to the edge of the map which had become rather dog-eared from a previous corner crease. Now it looked like their most direct route to Dieppe.

"Maybe we'll come across some other units on the main road?" Rutherford was referring to one of the big 'coast' roads that linked Paris with France's northern coastal towns.

"OK. I'm with you on that." Stock used the opportunity to loosen the fuel tank filler and peer into the gloomy space to see how much fuel they had used and decided they would have to top up their tanks before much longer. "Which way here?"

"Take the left fork, then it's about another five miles to the main road and the bridge should be just beyond. That town off to the right's Saint Riquier, so we don't want that."

'Not much of a main road,' thought Stock as they pulled up at a dog-leg junction, but he could see the bridge next to a church just off to their right. Nobody, no traffic, nothing to indicate that anyone else was venturing outside but, worryingly, no army units either. He remembered reading somewhere in his field manual that bridges offered the key to any successful campaign yet this one was deserted. Perhaps they were all off at the front line well behind them, he pondered. With a nod to Day who had pulled up on his left, he gunned the engine and crossed the flat road towards the bridge. 'Not much of a bridge either,' he thought as they passed a sign that announcing 'La Somme', the river made famous by the Great War a quarter of a century earlier.

A few miles later they crossed the flat basin through which the Somme meandered, and approached the town of Oisemont, Stock could at last see people and vehicles in the distance, but it was particularly awkward to make out who they were and what was happening as the sun was now directly in his eyes. It was only at the last moment before they came to a stop did he recognise another British uniform, and then only because the chap was standing in the long shadow of a truck straddling the road. They parked the BSAs off to one side and Stock walked up to the man who he could now see held his rifle across his body, but he was not challenged.

"Who are you?"

The tall man came to attention. "Private Gritton, 4562456, sir." He was smartly dressed but from his attitude and dress, clearly on sentry duty in the field.

"Where's your CO?"

"Sergeant Gritton behind the truck, sir."

"OK. Carry on." Stock went to go behind the truck but paused when he realised he had been given the same name. "Two Grittons, Private?"

"Yes, sir, not related, though. You'll see what I mean." The wide smile reminded Stock of Day's.

He chose to go round the front of the truck and, in a small depression ahead of him in the road, saw a British tank with several men milling around. It was one of the newer, heavily armoured tanks which carried a bigger gun and was affectionally known as a Matilda. He was to find out later that Matilda was actually its official name and wonder who would name a tank after a woman.

One of the men holding a large spanner stopped what he was doing when he saw him approach, nudging another on the ground underneath the rear of the tank with his boot.

"Sergeant Gritton?" The nudger indicated with a double tap of his boot to the prostrate chap who took his time to emerge. He was covered in so much mud it was difficult to see where his eyes were, even after he had wiped a cloth over his face.

"Who's asking?"

"Second Lieutenant Stock, Royal Engineers, is asking. Are you Sergeant Gritton?"

"Normally yes, but right now I'm the only man round here who can fix this bloody thing. Give me a couple of minutes and we can get moving." He didn't wait for a response but disappeared back under the tank again.

Stock had not been this close to a tank before and took the opportunity to walk round it, admiring the size, shape, and the sheer ferocity it exuded. He had been told about these new tanks on the officers' training course in case a bridge had to be constructed. He remembered that they weighed 27 tonnes and carried three men, but, oh, so slowly. It was heavier at the back than the front due to its twin engines which did not counter-balance the long 2 pounder gun that normally protruded forwards. As with all new machines, it had its pros and cons; while it was loved by its crews, the newly invented suspension was cursed by them. Perhaps that was what they were working on at the moment, Stock mused as he spotted a useful looking 50 calibre Vickers machine gun poking out from the turret. By the time he had nearly come full circle, he found Sergeant Gritton standing in front of him, wringing his hands in a cloth.

"Fixed - for the moment. Now, what can I do for you, sir?" He had a definite Scottish accent and Stock could see what the other Gritton had meant by them not being related; this wiry man was about half the height of the first Gritton and really did not look anything like his namesake.

"Problems with your bogey wheels, Sergeant?" Stock's keen eye had not missed the size of the spanner the other man held and had a good idea where it might fit.

Gritton was surprised at the question, wondering how a second lieutenant from the Royal Engineers would know about such exact things, unless he had been attached to another tank regiment. "Aye. It's the bloody Woodruff keys that keep shearing, but we've made our own shaped drift that means we can knock the old one out and tap a new one into place without taking the whole thing off." He waited for a smarter retort to see to what extent this officer knew his onions in case it had been a lucky guess.

Even though Stock knew precisely what he was talking about, having experienced similar problems with the farm tractors, he was more interested in their current situation, and wasn't about to waste time discussing the finer points of mechanical engineering on a deserted road somewhere in northern France. Besides which, the sun had just set, and daylight was fast receding, making it very difficult to navigate much further through the French countryside.

"We're en route to Dieppe. Evacuation from Dunkirk is now impossible but we think it is still possible from Dieppe. Which unit are you with and what are your orders, Sergeant?"

"Evacuation? Nobody told us about any evacuation," he exclaimed and looked round, without success, at his fellows to see if they had heard of any such rumour. "What evacuation, sir?"

Stock told the gathering assembly what he had been told by Major Wavertree back at the airfield: that the Germans were now surrounding Calais and Dunkirk. "It seems we are being pushed west. Dieppe and Le Havre appear to be the nearest ports open to us. Do you mean to tell me that you don't know about this?"

"Our radio has been useless ever since we left Boulogne and we haven't heard anything since yesterday morning. We're part of G Battalion and supposed to be catching up with the 51st Highland Division at Amiens. That's G battalion of the 7th Royal Tank Regiment and this is one of our support vehicles." He nodded towards the truck behind Stock. "But these bloody bogey wheels are taking turns to jam up so we're well behind them now."

It was getting dark, and Stock really did not relish the prospect of getting lost in it. "Are you going on tonight?"

Gritton looked round beyond his tank. "Probably best not to now. There's no cover out here but we came through a small town just back there, so we'll camp in an empty barn I spotted. There's everything we need in the truck and you're welcome to join us."

It turned out that there were two slatted barns that abutted the road and fitted the bill perfectly. They chose the larger of the two. It could almost have been the start of the town of Oisemont; a hundred yards further on, the first of the more solid buildings started and Stock could see the glimmer of lights here and there. Sergeant Gritton had ordered the Matilda off to one side and his men set about making camp at one end using the headlights from the truck to pierce the gloom and make a fire. By the speed of their progress, it was a routine they were well used to. Day had followed Stock into one of the barns on his BSA. Stock unbuckled one of his panniers as Day stalled his engine next to him.

"Let's top up our tanks tonight but wait until these chaps have got some other form of lighting going. I don't fancy going up in smoke twice in one day," he said. It was notoriously difficult to pour petrol from the two-gallon cans without it glugging and splashing everywhere; besides which, the exhausts were still hot.

It took less than half an hour before Gritton's men had assembled round the fire to cook and eat from their mess tins, but Stock's party didn't have any rations.

"Oh. That's not a problem," declared Gritton. "There's enough in that wee truck to last a month. Help yourselves to some of Scotland's finest bully beef." He leaned over and handed Stock a satchel half-full of tins. " I noticed the locals have got their chickens locked away. Can't blame them really. Spooner here loves chicken - they must have known he was coming."

Gritton's men nodded in silent humour but the youngest blurted out, "I'll go and catch another one for you if you like, Spoons."

"You mention bloody chickens again and I'll shove one down your throat," Spooner growled.

"Better still, I'll go and catch one for him. I'd love to see a chicken in place of his ugly mug," another offered, and they all laughed, except for Spooner whose name had been shortened to Spoons - a happy coincidence of name and appearance since his face somehow resembled a big dessert spoon.

There were six of them in Gritton's party and brief introductions were made. "It was his birthday last week, so we caught a couple of chickens to celebrate, and the lads made a pillow from the feathers for him but left the gizzards in it. Ha! Stank to high heaven after a couple of days and it took him another couple to find out where the smell was coming from."

To Stock's mind, this was a happy crowd, but he wanted to find out more about what was happening. "What's the last thing you heard over the radio?"

"Ian here was on it at the time….tell them, Ian!" Gritton was intent on eating; so were the others but he used his prerogative to carry on while others did the talking. "He's our radio wizard and general know-it-all, aren't you, Ian? Can't fix the bloody thing though, can you?"

Corporal Ian didn't rise to the challenge. "Not much to tell, really. They're only short wave sets and don't have much range, but I've got a mate who was with the Captain up the front of the column when he overhears the radio from the Colonel's bigger set saying that we were pushing the Jerries back near a place called Cambrey…or Cumbray." He paused to swallow and put another half-forkful into his mouth. "We're stationed up near Boulogne expecting to be ordered off in that direction and we end up coming down here. We're supposed to be in Amiens right now."

Gritton decided to ask what they were all wanting to ask, "Do you think we ought to carry on to Amiens or follow you, sir?"

Stock knew this was coming and had his answer ready, but he waited to give the impression he was thinking it over, "I think you should follow your orders, Sergeant."

The brief silence was only compounded by the hissing fire. For all he knew, there was a railhead at Amiens ready to take this tank battalion to wherever it was needed, and as a mere second lieutenant had no authority to order otherwise. He had his orders and they had theirs and that was how the British army worked: by following orders.

"I think you should catch up with your column at Amiens as soon as you can and report to your CO. If anything's changed, I am sure he'll tell you. Just because we've been ordered to evacuate doesn't mean that you have," Stock continued.

"But what about those bloody Stukas? We got nothing to fire back at them," piped up Spooner. They had all heard the news about the dive bombers that had virtually wiped out the French armour a few days earlier. It was the one thing that a tank crew could do nothing about.

"And your Matildas frighten the hell out of the Germans so don't let a few aircraft put you off. Besides which, you wouldn't have been ordered to Amiens unless there was some AA there, would you?" Stock knew very well how frightening those Stukas were, but he didn't want to demoralise this group. "Sun rises about five o'clock around here, so we'll move off at 04.30. Ok with you, Sergeant?" He didn't have to ask but he felt it better to keep on the good side of Gritton. Just in case.

"Here, I've got something for you chaps." He returned from his BSA a few second later. "Have some cheese with the compliments of the Royal Engineers."

"Hooray for the Royal Engineers," piped up one.

"Gives me the trots," volunteered the youngest.

Stock went outside to relieve himself. When he returned, he found Gritton waiting for him by the entrance. "Just to let you know, sir, I've set sentry watch at three hours. I've got the first and Rodgers the second. What about yon civilian, Mr. Rutherford, I mean? I'll need to know who he is for my report."

"He's attached to us and we're escorting him back to England. I think that's all you need to know." Stock wasn't about to start making up stories and consequentially put himself in an awkward position.

"Just thought I'd ask, sir, as I've noticed that he hasn't let that briefcase out of his sight. As long as you know what you're doing, sir. Hope you don't mind me pointing that out."

"Thank you, Sergeant." He realised that Gritton was intimating that there might be black market items within and was inferring that both Stock and Day were also involved. He very quickly discarded the thought of haranguing Gritton for suggesting such a thing, but he had to admit that to an outsider, it was a distinct possibility.

"One favour sir. If you do get back to England and we don't, I have an older brother I haven't seen for a couple of years now. He's in the HAC and he's the reason why I joined up. If you're in London, could you look him up and give him my best wishes? Oh, and tell him I'm still happily single."

Stock had never been to the Honourable Artillery Company's headquarters which lay just north of the City. He was thrilled at the prospect of having a valid excuse as he had heard it was a magnificent building. called 'The In and Out Club' but didn't know why and now he'd have the chance to find out. "I'll be glad to, Sergeant. What's his first name?"

"Captain Alec Gritton, sir. Looks a bit like me, but then I suppose he would, wouldn't he?"

"Why do they call it the 'In and Out'?"

Gritton smiled and turned his head slightly. "I'll let him tell you that, sir."

Stock grinned. "See you in the mornings, Sergeant."

"Good night, sir."

"Oh, by the way, what's your first name?"

"Angus. Angus Conan Gritton from Perth."

The rest of them were settling down for the night. Gritton's comments about the briefcase had set him off wondering again. He still hadn't had a proper explanation. He seized the opportunity to corner Rutherford out of earshot of the others and ask, "You promised to tell me more about yourself, remember?"

He could see Rutherford wavering and pushed a little harder. "Look, if we're going to make it to Dieppe, sooner or later we're going to come across one of our roadblocks and I'm sure they won't let just anybody on a boat, so you'd better tell me what you're up to." He didn't add 'or you can start walking now'; he could keep that up his sleeve.

"Ok. But this is top secret stuff I'm about to tell you so it mustn't go any further. Really. I have your word?"

"Certainly."

Rutherford looked around to make sure nobody was eavesdropping before beginning, "I'm attached to the inventions section of the War Department and I was sent out to Paris to meet this chap who's found a crystal that, shall we say, improves transmission ranges. The admiralty has been dying to get hold of this for ages. When they found out there was a sample in Paris, they moved heaven and earth to get me out there and bring it back. It's here in this case along with all the paperwork and documents relating to its source, who holds rights in the invention and so on, as well as the specifications as to how to integrate it into the new sets."

He paused to let what he had just said sink in.

"I don't normally do this sort of thing, but our contact insisted that I met him personally just to make sure it went to the right place, and certainly not to the Germans. I was supposed to fly back to London directly but at the last minute we were diverted to Arras to pick up someone else - I don't know who - and were shot down before we got there. I've been trying to get across the Channel for several days now."

Stock pondered this for a few moments. "That's hardly a story we can tell the MPs when we get stopped. We need something else, so you'd better tell me more."

Rutherford took a slightly deeper breath, reached into his inside breast pocket, and retrieved a small red canvas booklet which he offered to Stock before beginning his explanation, "My name's Robert Rutherford, Rubby to my friends, you see."

"My cousin is Ernest Rutherford, inventor of an advanced form of underwater radar called ASDIC. He and this other chap from Switzerland called Miltz, the contact I was meeting, claim to have found a way to make it all work properly. I was working on it at our end in our laboratories in Portsmouth under Admiral Godfrey, but we kept getting interference from the metal hulls of the ships. We tried everything: minesweepers with wooden hulls, towing it with a rope hawser, tried a yacht once and even a barrage balloon, but we still came up with static, even with it all fully insulated.

He patted the case and craned his head nearer. "This crystal can be tuned to cut out that interference, making submarine and mine detecting much easier. At the moment we're lucky if we can get a clear reading at a hundred feet. This can read subs at half a mile, maybe more.

"I was asked to go to Paris to meet Miltz as I've met him on a couple of occasions, so was someone who he knew he could trust. These crystals are bloody heavy when you've got to lug them around half of France. Here, feel this!"

Stock took the benign looking case with his other hand and was surprised just how heavy and dense it felt.

Rutherford - Rubby - paused to swallow and then continued, "If the Germans get hold of this before we get our sets operational, we'll have the devil's own job playing catch up. But if we can get the drop on them, well, you can see the benefits. They sent me by plane instead of by boat just because of the minefields outside Calais harbour. They're laying new ones faster than we can detect them, even with our minesweepers going flat out.

"Perhaps you can see now why I didn't have time to tell you all this before and how important it is that I get back to England. There's only me and two others in the country who know how this works. It'll only be a matter of days before we can have the first set going."

Stock could see the gravity of it all and felt for Rutherford. He angled the red booklet towards the fire so he could see Rutherford's photograph and noted that it was stamped WD, the seal of the War Department, in bold red letters. He felt more reassured. "I think this ought to get us through but in case it doesn't, do you have anything else to show them?"

"Of course not! This is supposed to be top secret. I do have a couple of names I can refer them to, but they'll be back in England."

"Our best will have to be good enough then, won't it?" He handed the booklet back to Rutherford. "Can I see the crystals?"

"Don't see why not but it's a bit dark in here. I'll show you tomorrow."

"Done! You kipping here?" Stock pointed to spot behind a wooden upright.

"Yes, see you at 4.30!"

Stock left him to it and made his way over past the BSAs without tripping over the unseen straw that lay around. 'I really need some sleep' he told himself as he propped himself in a corner, but instead he found himself reflecting upon the previous days' events.

Only two days ago, he had been just another junior officer on his first posting, blissfully unaware that the army - of which he was part - was about to make the biggest evacuation in its history. He remembered his first day when he arrived at Frévent: he presented himself to Major Wavertree in one of the huts and was asked what he was good at. When he explained that he had lived on a farm for most of his life but enjoyed building, with a grin on his face, the Major stood up, shook him by the hand and gave him his first job: constructing a block of latrines.

"The open sewer is stinking out the Officers' Mess. Make it go away and I'll stand you in for a round," promised the Major.

He wasn't exactly a laughingstock, but an officer straight out of training school detailed to work on the latrines was too good a target to miss. He could sense the men sniggering behind his back and decided he had to make his mark and earn their respect.

The opportunity was there almost immediately as the company under him had been complaining of loose bowels. Several times throughout the next day when they had been felling trees for timber, one man or another would disappear further into the wood to relieve himself. An obnoxious odour hung over the long table where they sat and ate their evening rations; tock had noticed an abnormal number of flies buzzing around.

That evening he requisitioned a tin of red dye, normally reserved for marking out bays and the like, from the NAAFI stores, and tipped it along the trench that served as a toilet for some two hundred men, all the while keeping his mouth shut so that the swarms of flies didn't get into it. He then had a word with the orderly and told him to lay out extra rations on the table well before they next sat down.

When it was time to eat, Stock stood back a little and watched with amusement as the men congregated round the table, commenting upon the feast in front of them. From his perspective, he could see that the heat of the afternoon had done its job. It took all of one minute before one chap questioned what the numerous red dots on the corned beef were. Stock brought them to silence, lined them up, marched them over to the open ditch, and made them look down into the trench. The foul sight of tens of thousands of flies feasting on their dyed faeces had the desired effect. He kept them at attention while he explained that that was where the red dots had come from, carried by the flies which left the trench to explore the food on the table. The men had been eating their own excrement . He didn't need to keep them there much longer; it was evident he had made his point as soon as one chap doubled over and vomited.

That had been a good day and only his second at that. He smiled at the memory, closed his eyes, and slept.

It didn't seem like he had been asleep for more than five minutes when he felt his foot being gently kicked by Corporal Day; he knew Stock didn't take long to be up and about and had left him to sleep as long as possible. "Just about four-fifteen, sir. Tea?"

Stock gratefully took the offered mug while he watched the outline of Gritton's men moving around outside in the half-light. First the truck's engine came to life, its headlights swinging away from the barn entrance as it moved away, followed by the louder roar of one of the Matilda's engines. He sat for a while mulling over what Rutherford had revealed to him the night before and decided he would do everything he could to get the man and his case back to England. He'd studied the map yesterday and assessed they were about 40 miles from Dieppe - say a couple of hours. All they needed to do was to get through this town and generally head west. No need for any fancy shortcuts if only Rutherf...

BANG! An almighty explosion just outside brought the other side of the barn down inwards, followed by heat and flames. Dust and smoke prevented him from seeing anything much, but he felt a familiar wetness between his thighs. 'Damn! I've spilt my tea' he thought.

BANG! Another explosion, this one a bit further away. 'Bloody Hell, it's those ruddy Stukas again.'

BANG! This time, he felt more than saw the truck disappear in a blinding ball of fire through the slats that made up the outside barn walls. He tried to decide whether to stay down or jump on the BSA and run. Both Day and Rutherford were half-buried under a pile of timbers and smouldering straw.

"Let's get out of here," he shouted to them. "Come on! Move!" Logic told him that they would make relatively unworthy targets out in the open when compared to the barn or the Matilda.

Day staggered to his machine, but Rutherford wasn't moving.

"Get him up, Corporal!"

As Day pulled the man upright he could see that Rutherford had a blood-soaked face and in the flickering light also saw that he was unconscious. "Put him across my tank! Let me get on first."

Whoosh, bang! This time it wasn't an explosion. Stock peered through the slats to see that it was the Matilda that had fired its gun just as Day managed to get Rutherford straddled across Stock's fuel tank. 'What the hell are they firing at?' thought Stock as he adjusted the choke and kick started his BSA. He leaned over to retrieve Rutherford's briefcase from the ground and jammed it between them.

Almost tipping the bike over in his hurry to turn it round, he vacated the burning barn as quick as he could. Day was right behind him, and they headed for the nearest building across the field behind the barn. Both of them had to swerve at the last second to miss a small ditch.

BANG! It wasn't until they were well past the second stone building did Stock stop them and look back. Black earth was raining down on the Matilda as it trundled its way in the direction that they had come from the previous night. The truck exploded a second time as its cargo of fuel and spare ammunition caught; Stock hoped that whoever was in that truck at the time hadn't felt anything.

Whoosh, bang! The Matilda's gun fired again. They all peered into the distance to see what it was firing at, but it was not quite light enough for them to make anything out. Watching the Matilda was quite a stirring sight as it trundled across the field into the jaws of an unseen enemy, and he briefly thought it would make a splendid patriotic picture. Stock looked up into the sky hoping there weren't any Stukas about. It was empty of everything except a flock of startled crows off to his left. Someone had fired on them from ground level and very effectively too; the only enemy Stock could think of would be a German army unit and he was amazed that they had come this far so quickly.

He was still partly stunned himself and, now that they were relatively safe, had time to muster his thoughts; he looked down at Rutherford's prone body in front of him and saw how close his hands were to the hot exhaust.

"Up you get!" he muttered and carefully levered Rutherford's chest, but the body kept on going and collapsed in a heap on the gravel between the two bikes. The briefcase landed next to him. His eyes were open and unblinking. There was a nail protruding from his temple. One look from Day confirmed what Stock already knew; he was dead.

"Damn. What the blazes are we going to do now?" he groaned. He could hear more shells landing around the Matilda, even though she was now out of sight and thought he heard her returning fire but just then he caught sight of Germans half-tracks moving towards the town from another road off to the South. He assessed their situation as quickly as he could. 'Those half-tracks carry troops. We can't just leave Rutherford's body here; questions will be asked as to who he is, not only by the townspeople but also the Germans if they find him. That's probably the last thing we want them to know. If the town is surrounded, then we won't be able to get out either and Rutherford's crystals won't get back to England. On top of that, we'll be captured.'

"Give me a hand, Corporal," he grunted as he leaned over to replace Rutherford back on the fuel tank, while handing the case to Day. "Follow me."

They didn't have far to go and stopped by one of the craters made by the German shells, Stock estimated about seventy paces from the partly scorched tree closest to the now blazing barns and truck. Day could see what Stock had in mind and helped him carry the body into the shallow crater.

"Get that shovel - quickly now!" Stock ordered. He had nearly run over it when escaping from the barn a few minutes earlier. Presumably, it had been thrown clear from the truck when it had exploded the first time. He didn't know how much time they had before there would be Germans running all over the place, but he knew it couldn't be long. Out of the corner of his eye he saw a flash of light, followed by a boom and hoped it wasn't the Matilda.

They dug quickly. Luckily, the earth was soft. Before they lowered Rutherford's body into his grave, Stock knelt down and rifled through his pockets, retrieving amongst other things the WD booklet. Before Day started shovelling the earth back, he picked up the case and tossed it into the grave as well. If they couldn't get out of here, he didn't want Rutherford's secrets falling into enemy hands. But then he had second thoughts: 'What if everything Rutherford had told him was all a big lie just so that he could get back to England? Suppose there were no crystals?'

"Hold on a minute!" he said to Day, who stopped his shovelling while Stock hopped down onto the soft ground around Rutherford, brushed off some earth, and snapped open the two case latches. Rather gingerly, not knowing what to expect, he opened it and stared down at mess of rocks, most about the size of a small cricket ball but some larger and flatter with rough edges. They were pale and almost flinty in appearance but not like anything he had come across before. He chose a smaller one and put it in his pocket. Bunched up underneath this self-contained quarry was a sheaf of papers. He chose one leaf at random, folded it, and put it in another pocket.

Five minutes of hard work - Day with the shovel, Stock with his hands - produced a passable but inconspicuous grave, as well as a sweat. They stood up, exhausted. It was then that Stock realised he had not heard any more artillery fire for a while. 'Perhaps it was the Matilda and if it was, the enemy would soon be upon them,' he thought.

"That'll do. Let's go!" he ordered Day.

"Which way, sir?"

"Round the town to the north." This would take them away from where he had seen the half-tracks approaching. "Then we go west."

Chapter 5

Dieppe

As far as Stock was concerned, the race was on. If they could reach the coast before the Germans, they ought to be able reach Dieppe, and if not… Well, he didn't want to think about the consequences.

The loud exhausts of the bikes reverberated off the buildings. As much as they tried, they couldn't find a road round the town, and they found themselves having to negotiate the narrow lanes on the outskirts. Stock could see the sunrise on his right and was thankful that he now had some light to help. At least he could navigate more quickly - stopping to check where they were on the map was not a practical option and he hadn't had time to memorise any name places before they set off.

This town was similar to the others they had passed: brick town houses with half-rendered facades, wooden shacks, unkempt weed-strewn plots, roads that merged with pavements. They all melded into one. He had been looking for the tell-tale church spire that normally marked the approximate middle of a town, but he hadn't seen it yet, and he was beginning to think they were heading unwittingly into the town centre when he spotted a wider road off to their right. This road seemed to want to take them in the direction they were trying to go.

Relieved, they broke into open countryside and opened their throttles, until they came to a fork by a barn. Stock prudently stopped in its shadow, Day besides him. After looking over his shoulder, pulled out the map.

"I reckon we're either here, or there. There's a main road ahead somewhere and we've still one more river to cross- here, at

Gamaches. If that one's been taken by the Germans, we'll go like hell along the east bank until we find a bridge that isn't. OK?"

"I'll be right behind you, sir," Day replied cheerfully.

The straight roads undulating through the open French countryside were just what they needed to put as much space between themselves and the Germans as possible, although Stock couldn't go much over sixty. Every time he did, there was a nasty vibration that felt like it was coming from the rear wheel. Even so, it didn't take them long to reach Gamaches. This time, as they crested a rise Stock could see the central church spire and headed for it when the roads allowed. His logic proved right, and they turned left onto the road that led to the river. And stopped.

No more than fifty feet in front of them was a roadblock made of wooden blocks and barbed wire and manned by several soldiers, all of whom were looking their way. British soldiers armed and ready. Stock and Day coasted up to it and turned off their BSAs.

"Identify yourselves," an aggressive voice shouted.

Stock looked to his left and saw a sergeant pointing his rifle at them. At first he was taken aback as he felt that they must surely be recognised as Royal Engineers, but then realised that in their current state of dress, they could very well have been anyone. He had long since lost his cap and their torn uniforms were covered with mud, ash and blood, hiding the insignia badges on their arms. Had he known it, their hidden faces behind split goggles looked as though they had just emerged from a camouflage factory and, on top of that, they were on BSAs when Royal Engineers usually travelled by Jeep. Despite the just visible single 'pip' on his shoulders designating his rank of second lieutenant, there was just one saving grace; they didn't have Rutherford with them.

Formalities were exchanged and the men relaxed, though the sergeant quite rightly insisted on inspecting their warrant cards.

"Not to put too finer a point on it, sir, but you both look like you've come from hell," he commented. It was the sergeant's way of asking where they had come from, and why.

Ever since the previous night when Rutherford had enlightened him about his secret, along the way from Oisemont Stock had been considering his answer to just such a question, since he knew it would be asked of him sooner or later. He had not had a chance to discuss this with Day and, if asked, hoped he would not mention Rutherford. He explained that their basic orders were to evacuate, and that Dieppe was their goal. He would have a word with Day the first chance he got, once they were across this bridge.

Stock wanted to find out about Dieppe. He asked in reply, "You obviously haven't been ordered out yet, have you?"

"No, sir. Our orders are to man this roadblock and observe," he confirmed and then glanced up at the top of the church spire. "And in case you're wondering, I posted a man up there and we saw you coming ten minutes ago." He was grinning a little as if to prove that they were doing their job properly. Stock had seen the observer corps shoulder flashes on their uniforms and looked up to see a rifle poking out of the church spire.

An idea came into his head. "Are you in radio contact with Dieppe, then?" Perhaps he could get them to warn other roadblocks of their approach and ease their passage.

"No, sir, only with the bridge on the other side of town via a runner. Dieppe's too far away, but the CO might be able to help. Oi, Shifty! What's the name of the place where the CO is?" he shouted across the street.

"O."

"What?"

"O."

"I said what's the name of…"

"I heard you, Sarge. It's called 'O'- spelt Eu," Shifty said for the third time as he wandered over to join them.

The sergeant turned to Stock to explain, "Shifty's sister married a Frog from somewhere around here and speaks the lingo. Can't get round it myself so why bother, eh?"

Stock wondered what use an observer detachment was if it could only observe without having the ability to report their observations quickly. He weighed up warning them about the advancing Germans against his need to get to Dieppe quickly and decided not to interfere. After all, they probably weren't about to take orders from a junior lieutenant from another regiment.

"Which is the quickest road to Dieppe?" he asked.

"Shifty," prompted the sergeant.

Private Shift scratched his head under his beret for a moment before starting to explain, "There's a long way and there's a short way but if I were you I'd go across country if you've got a map. Go down this road, turn right in about a mile, then take the next left and keep going for another, oh, five or six miles. Then… I'm not really sure after that. Only been here once before and then it was some years ago. My sister was getting married and…"

"That'll do, Shifty. Can't expect anyone to remember everything can you, sir?" He was keeping Shifty in his place. "We've been here two days now and I can tell you we came from that direction from Dieppe. Just dropped off with only a day's worth of rations and this piece of rubbish that we had to put together. Wouldn't stop a child on a bike, let alone any Jerries," he said bitterly and kicked the flimsy wooden cross that suspended one half of the roadblock, rattling the barbed wire that looked like it was the only thing keeping it all together.

'Stopped us,' thought Stock.

"Thank you, Sergeant. Carry on - and good luck!" Stock returned the sergeant's salute before walking back to the bikes. Day was now the only one in earshot, so he hissed, "Listen! I think it better if we're stopped again that we don't mention Rutherford. It'll only slow things up. OK?"

"As you say, sir."

Stock studied the map, trying to memorise as many name places as he could so they wouldn't have to keep stopping. Shifty and another pushed the roadblock to one side, just enough for them to pass onto the stone bridge which had several humps to it and extended for several hundred yards. They followed Shifty's advice easily enough, taking the road up out of the wide valley. Stock kept them heading north and west when he could as he didn't want to run the risk of coming across any Germans that had penetrated further than their last encounter.

Just half an hour later, having passed through several small villages through the slightly hillier countryside, Stock consulted the map at a multiple fork next to a decrepit water tower. The sun behind them was becoming a watery orb in the heavy gathering cloud and the previously helpful shadows were starting to merge into one another. He had just decided which route to take and was about to engage the clutch, when over the idling engines they both heard the drone of aeroplane engines. Stock knew that pilots' navigators relied upon landmarks to find their way around and he was a little surprised that there were aircraft flying in such poor visibility. Nevertheless, a flight of several twin-engine bombers accompanied by the inevitable Stukas came into sight from behind them at low level. In fact, they were so low that he was worried that any one of their machine gunners might decide to use them as target practice. In a few seconds they were gone, heading for the town of Dieppe which Stock was hoping they would be able to see just over the next rise.

"Come on!" he shouted at Day as he released the clutch. They're probably using the same road as we are as their marker."

It wasn't much of a rise but when Stock paused them, they could make out the predictable church tower, but their attention was focussed on the spectacle of destruction as the bombers dropped their cargoes. Black smoke was already dissipating into the low cloud which refracted an orangish light from below, accompanying brighter flashes of exploding bombs and targets. Even though they had kept their engines running, they could clearly hear the crumps and booms, each one un-attributable to any specific flash due to sound delay. Identifiable machine gun fire both from the air and ground interjected the brief silence between explosions and they sensibly stayed where they were, helplessly watching the bombers as they finished their runs. The smaller Stukas buzzed around the port, like flies eyeing up their next meal, before diving on their next quarry.

It was a depressing spectacle and Stock hoped there would still be boats capable of evacuation. He had not seen or heard any evidence of heavy calibre anti-aircraft fire and was wondering if those guns had been the first victims, if indeed there had been any in the first place. All of a sudden it was over, and the fleet of bombers was coming directly over their heads, using the same road as their marker to return to base. With horror, it dawned on Stock that they were in full view and made perfect targets in the middle of a straight road. Just in time he released the clutch and his BSA leapt forward. He could hear Day on his machine right behind him. Should have asked him to keep watch, he berated himself. This time, there was no hedge, no big trees, water tower, barn or church they could hide behind, only an orchard some hundred feet to their left; it wouldn't hide them completely, but it was their only option, so they took to the track that crossed the ditch as bullets whacked into the soft earth next to them. Stock was going too fast and had to swerve violently and duck down to avoid hitting the first of the small apple trees. His heavy BSA didn't take too kindly to the kind of manoeuvres he was demanding of it, but he managed to miss the first tree and was about to negotiate the next when he heard a loud 'CLANG,' then another 'CLONG' The bike threw itself sideways and toppled him to the ground between two tree trunks without giving him the chance to right it. He didn't have time to cry out from the pain in his leg which was trapped beneath the sliding machine before he saw Day's front wheel ride over his outstretched hand, followed immediately by the rear wheel which somehow, mercifully, missed it. Then it all went quiet. Then he felt the pain in his leg again and recognised the smell of burning fabric.

'Hot exhaust, must move.' His survival instincts galvanised him into levering the heavy bike up enough to retrieve his leg from under it and he pushed himself a mere two feet to prop himself against number two tree. Inspecting his right leg just below the knee, he found that part of the BSA had ripped a line across his trouser which was covered in oil. Blood slowly oozed from a narrow gash. He flexed his knee and kneaded it to feel whether it would hold his weight and decided it probably would.

Day came panting into sight. "You alright, sir?"

Stock then felt the ache in his right hand and ceased his massaging to look at it. "Between you and the Germans I think I'll live." He held it up so Day could see the faint outline of a tyre imprint on the back of it together with a torn nail on his little finger dangling by a sinew.

It took Day a moment to realise why Stock was showing it to him. "Sorry, sir. Did my best to miss you when you fell."

"I didn't fall. The bike was shot out from under me. Have a look at it, will you."

While Stock used the tree to help himself up, Day righted the BSA and immediately saw a small puddle of oil beneath it, dripping from the engine casing. He gasped, "You were very lucky, sir! Looks like a bullet's smashed through the crank case. Must have missed you by inches. How's your leg?"

Stock hobbled over to inspect it but didn't bend down. "Right where my leg was. Bloody Jerries!" One of the panniers had been ripped from its strapping and had a hole torn in it from end to end and he could see where another bullet had smashed into the rear wheel. "If yours is in a better state, you'd better go and get it."

"Mine's fine, sir," Day beamed, and then thought better of beaming when he saw the look on Stock's face. "Be right back, sir. Er, I think you might need my handkerchief again. You're bleeding from your cheek," he added with concern in his voice.

Stock refused the hanky and went to retrieve his goggles from the ground. One of the lenses was smashed and smeared with blood so he decided to leave them where they lay. He walked stiffly to the edge of the orchard where it met the road and heard Day's machine fire up, all the while exercising his leg and looking towards Dieppe. For some reason he stopped and inspected the budding fruit just before he crossed the ditch and noted that there was an extraordinary number of ripening apples on each branch, far more than the orchards he had known in England. 'Wonder what they taste like? Perhaps I'll live long enough to find out one day. Bloody Jerries!' He tugged sharply at his torn nail to free it.

He no longer needed the map as they had almost reached the edge of Dieppe. In any case, the billowing black smoke would lead them straight to where they wanted to go. Day pulled up next to him on the tarmac and Stock climbed onto the back half of the saddle. "You take it….my leg's a bit sore. Head for the right-hand smokestack!" He referred to one of several sources hoping that the furthest was nearer the sea-going docks.

Within a couple of minutes, they were in the outskirts of the port. For the first time since they had left the Frévent airfield, they saw a significant number of people and, a little further on, non-military vehicles going here and there. Stock tapped Day on the right shoulder to indicate the direction they should take at a crossroads and Day had to steer smartly out of the way of delivery truck that was bearing down on them. Before they realised it, they were having trouble seeing through the acrid smoke that clung on at ground level. Slowing down to a crawl by a tall wall, Day had to put his foot down to prevent the bike from toppling over. Crowds of people seemed to be scurrying in all directions. Then, from out of nowhere, two red capped soldiers appeared: MPs. 'That's all we need,' thought Stock. Trust the military police to be in the thick of a crisis.'

"YOU. DON'T STOP THERE. GET THAT MOTORBIKE DOWN THERE NOW!" Ignoring Stock, the bigger of the two with chevrons on his shoulder was shouting in Day's ear from less than three feet away and pointed to their left. Day picked his way through rubble and smouldering timbers and pulled up just short of a quay by a small crane. Right in front of them were several boats and ships, one of them sitting low in the water at the stern with smoke billowing from one of its air funnels. A twisted gangway sited nearer the front with one side missing had a mixture of people on it, mostly soldiers, all hurrying to get ashore, while some were jumping across the small gap between the rising and falling gunwales and the wharf. The assembling soldiers were being lead further down the cratered quayside and disappeared behind the smokescreen. Off to their left, a group of civilians was tugging on a large rope tied to a fishing vessel which was threatening to drift away in the current. The sound of part of a tall wall collapsing next to the crane made them flinch as bricks bounced around them like marbles being released from a paper bag. A scream pierced the already busy air, followed by shouting and the outline of running men visible through the smoke.

"Let's get down there!" shouted Stock and pointed off to their right.

Day took it very slowly as they passed the gathering company of soldiers, negotiating uneven and missing cobblestones interspersed with blocks of masonry until they cleared most of the foul smoke and they could see across to the other side of the harbour. It looked even more of a mess. Two small boats had capsized in tandem. Next to them what looked like an oiler was burning fiercely, its decks almost awash. A larger cargo ship was listing towards its moorings and the remains of a tugboat bobbed up and down, somehow still tethered to a floating pontoon in mid-channel. A fire crew with their decrepit equipment was losing the battle with a two-storey burning warehouse and from somewhere in the distance came the jangling bell of an ambulance. Wreckage from a toppled gantry lay across the bows of another ship, and a wooden bridge that had connected an island to the eastern side of the docks was on fire and had all but disintegrated.

"That chap there!" Stock had spotted an officer not far away who didn't seem to be panicking. He was deep in conversation with two sergeants. "Pull up next to him!"

Day stalled the BSA and Stock thankfully dismounted. It crossed his mind that this was what Rutherford had had to put up with for all those hours as a pillion passenger and his estimation of the determination of the man went up a notch.

"Sir!" Stock called out as he approached the captain from the side, came to attention and saluted. He winced from the pain in his right leg as he did so.

"Carry on, then, and try to keep that entrance clear." The captain finished his talk with the two sergeants who saluted and wheeled away in unison. He turned to Stock. As he went to return Stock's salute, he slowed visibly, taking in his appearance. What he saw made him drop his jaw. From the Germans' attack, he had already seen some injured men with horrific wounds and plenty of dead ones, but the second lieutenant who stood in front of him did not quite fit into that category. For a start, he was mostly covered with dirt when there wasn't any mud that he could recall around this side of the docks. Secondly, his face had the imprint of a man wearing goggles who had come through a swarm of flies. His blood encrusted hair was thick with grime, as was his tattered and stained uniform, but it was the haggard look on his face that had the captain wondering where this man had come from.

"How can I help you, Lieutenant?" he asked.

Stock didn't really know where to begin. He was about to state his rank and unit before asking where embarkation was taking place, when an almighty explosion knocked them all to the ground. It wasn't just one explosion but carried on and on, developing into what seemed an eternity of blasts. Day had landed mostly on top of him having been between him and the exploding ship. Stock could see spittle dribbling to the ground from his open mouth. Beyond him lay the prone figure of the captain. He wasn't sure if it was the heat or the shock waves that he felt first, but he remembered to cover his head with his arms and keep his mouth open. He was learning fast how to survive big explosions; by keeping an open mouth, he was less likely to have another perforated ear drum. He could feel the ground shaking and tried to bury himself further into the unyielding cobble stones as everything around him seemed to be coming apart.

Pieces of wood and metal rained down followed by hot embers. He dared not move. In any case, he didn't know in which direction he could move.

When the explosions started to subside, Stock decided it was becoming safe enough to hazard a look from under his own little shelter but there was too much smoke and dust to see further than a few feet. Then he caught the distinctive smell of cordite, wafting in waves. 'Ammunition ship, then,' he supposed as he sat up and smacked out his smouldering sleeve. He rubbed his hand over the back of his head as it was hurting. 'I'm getting fed up with this. Bloody Jerries.'

The acrid air cleared a little in the breeze and he could see all around him that there was hardly a foot of ground not covered with something that should not have been there, and that included bodies. The company of soldiers that they had passed now resembled wooden tops that had been mown down by a giant bowling ball. There was hardly any movement coming from them. The wall behind them where they had been standing delineated the docks from the rest of the town. It had been blasted into millions of pieces and now spread to the other side of the road. He gazed at where the smoking ship had been and recognised the back part of it; the front was nowhere to be seen. He had never seen such a mess and was having trouble comprehending how it had all come about. How had he got here? Why just here? When did he get here? Who are all these people? What was going on? What am I doing here? His haphazard thoughts were brought back into focus by another relatively small explosion from the ship and he turned to look for Corporal Day who lay face down, unmoving on the ground just behind him. Stock leaned over and shook his dusty frame, urging him to respond. "Corporal… Corporal?"

Day returned to consciousness. As he rolled over Stock could see that his face was covered with blood from a still bleeding nose. He also had a very bloodshot eye. The two of them just sat there facing each other, Stock weighing up their situation and Day coming to grips with what had happened.

"The last thing I remembered was seeing the back of your head coming towards me," Day rasped. He rubbed his sore eye, withdrew his hand and inspected the bright red blood on it. "How's your head, sir?"

Stock realised that it was the contact of Day's skull with his that was giving him a headache. "Not as colourful as the front of yours is going to be," he replied. They both managed a small grin. "See if the captain's alright, will you? You're nearest."

Day half-turned. "Captain…..Captain, sir?" There was no reply, so Day stood up and went to roll him over, tucking his arm in first. When he saw what was left of his face, it was clear that he was dead, and Stock watched the body slump onto its back. He shut his eyes but only for a moment. 'What a shame……Christ…..this is a real mess.'

"What do we do now, sir?"

'What indeed?' Stock was his officer and knew it was incumbent on him to make a decision, so he held his hand out to Day to help him to his feet.

Carefully picking their way through the rubble, they made their way back down the quay towards the company of soldiers who had been standing much closer to the blast. Those standing at the back had fared better than those at the front, although fared was not really an accurate description. To a man they had all suffered in one way or another and indeed it was only those who had been at the rear of the assembly who had survived; even then many of them were mutilated. Stock recognised one of the sergeants who had been addressed by the deceased captain and was glad to see he was standing and still had all his limbs. In the background, Stock could see civilians aimlessly wandering about, but now others were coming from the town, talking loudly and calling for friends and relatives. A woman stepped over one of the fallen redcaps, calling out and looking wildly around, followed by a young girl calling, "Mama!"

A group of about half-a-dozen men came running over the stump of the brick wall, stopped and just gawked at the scene until one chap pointed in the direction of the front of the ship and urged the others to follow him there. The stench of burning flesh was strongest next to where Stock stood and he took a few paces away rather than choke, but it all fused together with the bitter taste of oil and cordite as well as burnt paint and wood, adding up to a most unpleasant atmosphere. One soldier on all fours a few paces away was gagging and another was vomiting bile while loud coughs and moans came in every direction from those who were still capable of drawing air.

Stock decided they couldn't stay there and called out, "Sergeant?" The man didn't move so he went and stood in front of him and shouted, "SERGEANT!" The glazed look on the man's face said it all, but it dissipated as he started to take control of his senses.

"Sir?"

"Get what men you have to take the wounded further down the quay. By that boat," Stock ordered, arbitrarily choosing an untouched moored boat about a hundred yards away.

"Yes, sir!" the sergeant acknowledged but was still not moving.

"NOW!"

"Err… Yes, sir." At last, he started to attend to his orders.

Stock turned to Day and asked, "Give me a hand with this chap." He indicated a chubby soldier close by who was trying to get up but kept falling over. Stock could see why when they got him upright; his left ankle was turned at the wrong angle. The man let out a howl of agony as they lifted him and bore his weight between them so they could shuffle their way down the quayside to Stock's muster point. They leaned him against a metal stump. Turning round they saw what was left of the rest of the company straggling in their direction. Half of them were being helped by the other half of survivors. It was painful to watch their slow progress towards them. There were only about forty of them in all and Stock watched the sergeant bending down to check the fallen to see if any were still alive; he didn't envy him.

He approached two uninjured privates who were easing a man down to the ground. "You two, go and help the sergeant down there."

He was beginning to think about finding a vessel that would take them back to England and looked hopefully towards the end of the quay. It was empty except for a rusting old hulk of a cargo ship that looked more like it would sink if its mooring lines were released. Besides which, he hadn't a clue as to how to start an engine of something that size, let alone steer it. Beyond that and closer to the open sea he could see a much bigger ship, but that had obviously been hit by a bomb as it was listing over to one side.

He needed something straight away and he turned to the boat alongside them. It looked like a small passenger ferry and would easily take all of them. Whether or not it would make it across the channel was another matter, but he needed something and needed it right now. The shell-shocked men were clearly not up to anything much and they couldn't just stay where they were, and that applied to those who were still able to move about by themselves, let alone the injured. He went over to the edge of the quay and inspected the ferry. It was about sixty feet long with furled awnings around the hoops on the main deck. A small wheelhouse with an open back protruded nearer the front but one of its glazed panels was broken. Even if it was not designed to go out to sea, to Stock it looked capable and it was empty, and right next to them. Stock's only experience with boats had been when he had courted a girlfriend on the Norfolk Broads but that had been a much smaller boat.

Day was by his side so he suggested, "Do you think you can go and get our kit.....sharpish?" He turned to the company and asked, "Anyone here know anything about boats?"

His question was met with baleful stares that reminded him of a flock of sheep but after several seconds a man to his right put his hand up and said, "I do, sir." The man had a Devon accent.

Stock walked over to him and questioned, "Well?"

The man was bemused. "Used to work in a boatyard in Kingsbridge.....repairing yawls and the like." He looked worryingly around the dock as if this officer was going to ask him to start repairing things.

"Can you get that boat going?"

The man peered past Stock at the ferry before confirming, "Don't see why not, sir. It's just like any other boat."

"What's your name, Private?"

The soldier stood up straight and saluted before saying, "Elcombe, sir. Private James Elcombe, Royal Army Medical Corps."

"Well, Private, I'm Second Lieutenant Bernard Stock of the Royal Engineers and I'd like you to go and get that boat going." He saw the man waver at such an unusual order. "Do you think you can manage that?"

"I'll give it a go, sir." He still had a quizzical look about him, but Stock did not give him the chance to raise any queries, adding, "And check the fuel tank will you?"

The sergeant and two men were returning from their gruesome job empty handed, closely followed by Corporal Day.

"Sergeant, report?"

"All dead, sir. Even the two MPs the other side of the gate."

Stock wasn't surprised considering the size of the explosion. He considered their own good fortune that they had not been standing any closer, and then thought about the captain who had been right next to him and shuddered at the odds of having survived.

"Who's in charge here?"

"It looks like you are, sir. The Major and the other Lieutenant were aboard the ship when it went up. Captain Walker was standing next to you," replied the sergeant, his voice full of genuine sadness.

He decided it was time to introduce himself and repeated what he had told Elcombe. Then he asked what they were doing there.

"Sergeant Dunn, Royal Army Ordnance Corps, sir. Just came over from Southampton on a round trip last night and we were trying to unload the ship when the Jerries came over. No warning. Very worrying when you've got a ship load of ammunition. Tried to get everyone off but some stayed behind to keep it going and, well, you know the rest."

It wasn't what Stock wanted to hear but he got the gist of it and didn't pursue the sergeant for more of the grizzly details. "Didn't see any Engineers here when we arrived here, sir."

It was not a question, but it was clear from his inflected tone that he was asking what Stock was doing here. Stock obliged him, keeping the narration short and easily missing out Rutherford's involvement. As if on cue, there was the growl of an engine coming to life from the boat, followed by a belch of black smoke that hugged the water.

"We're returning to England, Sergeant. I asked one of your chaps to check the engine. Any objections?"

Dunn thought about it for a moment, comparing the small boat with the larger ones they were more used to. They were supposed to be returning to England after unloading but seeing that their ship was now resting on the bottom of Dieppe harbour and coupled with Stock's story about the Germans closing in, thought it the only option. "Not from me, sir, but I'm not sure all the lads can swim and then there's the injured. Are you sure it's big enough to get across the Channel, sir?"

"I really don't think we have much choice, Sergeant. Those Jerries we came across were right behind us two hours ago and they could be here any minute. What do you suppose…"

He was interrupted by the scurrying appearance from across the road of a shabby looking individual and a policeman, both of them shouting and gesticulating at them and the ferry. Stock immediately assumed that this was the owner of the ferry who had seen Elcombe successfully start his boat and was coming to back up his claim to his property with the help of a local policeman.

From the way his veins that stood out on his neck, the owner was obviously livid. He jumped aboard to confront Elcombe who was just emerging from a hatch, shouting as loudly as he could in the hope of intimidating the thief. The policeman recognised Stock as the man in charge and was gabbling away, inches from his face. Stock didn't understand a word of it but had a pretty good idea of what was being said. He wasn't going to let these Frenchmen deprive them of their one means of escape and decided that there was only one way to resolve the dispute. If he waited for a translation from God knows who, there would be bound to be others who would come to support their friends and then they would be stuck in this ruined port until the Germans arrived.

Looking first at Sergeant Dunn, who met his eyes, he held up his hand, palm away from himself and took one pace backwards. The policeman recognised the gesture and ceased his lecture. Stock slowly unholstered his revolver and pointed it at the policeman's midriff, remembering that he still hadn't reloaded it. Two seconds later, he heard Day cock his rifle with the bolt action but noted that it was pointed towards the policeman's feet, not at his head. 'Well done, Day,' he thought.

At the sound of Day's rifle being readied, the pair on the boat stopped their struggling. Stock knew that time was of the essence and that if he didn't impose his will upon the Frenchmen in the next few seconds, they would be trapped and probably arrested. There was no way he was going to give Day the order to shoot, and it wouldn't be long before the policeman realised that.

He stepped the one pace forwards so that his face was back in front of the policeman and poked his revolver in his stomach so that the threat was felt. "Go! Now!" He was desperately trying to remember the French word. "Alley! Now!"

The policeman was definitely worried and briefly looked at Sergeant Dunn but didn't receive any help there. He then looked over Stock's shoulder at the ferry owner, but he was in no position to help either. Stock jiggled his revolver a little more firmly and saw a surrendering look appear on his face; he had won. An unending stream of conversation rattled between the two Frenchmen, but Stock didn't wait for the outcome.

"Sergeant, get everyone on that boat and quickly. Corporal, get that chap off the boat."

The sergeant barked orders and the healthier ones helped their comrades over towards the boat; but the owner wasn't giving up and he threw punches at Elcombe who backed off and tripped over one of the mooring ropes. Day came up behind him and swung his rifle into the Frenchman's side, decking him in the process, yet the man still persisted in trying to stop his boat from being stolen, literally from under him. He twisted round and rose to a crouch to see that Day had reversed his rifle and was now pointing it at him, but in his hand was a knife. It was Sergeant Dunn who rescued the situation. He strode over to the Frenchman, grabbed his knife arm, and hauled him over the side into the water.

Stock had been watching the scene from dry land and had failed to notice that the policeman had disappeared from his side and was now running down the quayside between the thickening debris and disappearing into a cloud of smoke. He reckoned they had about three minutes at the most and he put his arm round one of the last stragglers to help him aboard.

"Private Elcombe," he shouted over the heads. "Get us out of here!"

Elcombe's head appeared through the throng. "Sir?"

"Get us out of here and be quick about it."

"Oh, OK, sir." He stepped round a couple of chaps in the direction of the wheelhouse before turning back to Stock. "You need to cast off, sir," he added, pointing in two different directions.

Stock was nearest the stern and looked down at the rope round the thick mooring post, bent down and started to untangle a knot he knew nothing about. With his damaged hands, it was taking far too long, and he looked to the front of the boat to see a similar knot. He saw he was being watched from the boat by one chap who was doing nothing to help. "Here, you!" he summoned the fellow. "Go and undo the front one." The private saw it was quicker to jump ashore to get to the front, rather than work his way down through the length of the boat. He had just managed to free the knot when Elcombe appeared and explained, "Make sure you toss it well on to the boat, otherwise it'll wrap itself round the prop." Stock threw him the rope and looked over to see the other chap doing likewise up the front before jumping the widening gap onto the ferry.

"Get going - out to sea!" he shouted to Elcombe and looked down the quay towards where the policeman had disappeared, only to see the owner dragging himself out of the water by some metal rungs. He could hear that Elcombe had engaged the engine and felt them move backwards and away from the quay and a few moments later the ferry started to move forwards with a rising engine note. He looked anxiously towards the sinking ship and saw the policeman emerge from the smoke with a group of men in tow. He could see that none of them was armed but one lucky shot might well put paid to his plans. Just in case, he called out to Corporal Day, "Make sure they can see you and keep your rifle ready."

The ferry had been moored pointing towards the inner harbour and Elcombe competently swung them around and opened the throttle a little more, heading towards the outer harbour. "Keep to the middle as much as you can," Stock suggested as he joined him in the wheelhouse."

To him, as a non-seagoing type, their progress seemed dreadfully slow as they passed an outcrop of rocks and a series of cliffs on their right where the harbour narrowed a little, but at last the open sea was in sight between the two arms of the outer harbour wall. He cast a glance behind them in case the owner had managed to obtain a faster boat but nobody else was in sight and he turned his attention to the men scattered around him. They lay and sat wherever there was space, but it was not in short supply, and he didn't think there was any danger of them being overloaded.

"Nice little boat," Day volunteered. Stock could see what he meant as it was obviously a well-kept vessel with evidence of fresh paint here and there. "Ought to get us back to England if the sea doesn't pick up too much."

Another thought came to Stock, and he addressed Elcombe, "Do you know where you're going?"

"Oh, that's easy, sir. North." He pointed at the simple control panel in front of him. "Can't navigate by the sun as it's too cloudy but there's a compass here, look. Not sure which port we'll make but I reckon it'll probably somewhere near Eastbourne as the Channel'll take us a bit to the east. Been sea fishing out of Exmouth several times and I know how fast the current can get but I haven't been this far south before. I reckon if we keep going north, we're bound to find England sooner or later, maybe by dark."

Stock had to grab hold of the side of the wheelhouse to keep upright as they approached the sea wall. "How's the fuel?"

"Plenty of fuel but it's the sea I'm worried about. This tub's not got much of a draught on it and if it gets rough then we might have to follow the sea, go with the wind." He could see that Stock knew nothing about boats but decided not to explain the consequences.

A noise from above and Stock looked up expecting an attack from the air, but it was nothing more than a flock of geese following the coastline. And that reminded him; he was hungry.

Chapter 6

Interview

"He's dead, sir," said a private who was hunched over a prone comrade whose arm terminated not much further below his shoulder, rivulets of his blood mapping out haphazard patterns across the wooden decking following the movement of the ferry. There was no need to close his eyes as they were already shut. Sergeant Dunn motioned for two others to stand up and use the tarpaulin they had been squatting on to cover the body.

"I don't think Crowell's going to make it either, Sarge," added the private. They looked across to see another man slouched against the side of the wheelhouse, head to one side with bloody dribble coming from the corner of his mouth and clutching at his stomach. He was completely still and his eyes were shut but he was just about breathing.

Once they were well clear of the harbour which had disappeared surprisingly quickly in the gathering cloud, Stock had learned little more from Sergeant Dunn other than that they had been detailed to escort supplies of all sorts back and forth across The Channel. They had had one more trip to go. The sergeant added, "I think the medical chaps were supposed to be going on from here, most of them youngsters, all except the captain. But most of them are now here." He looked around at the miserable bedraggled bunch. "They ought to be happy returning to England, but you wouldn't know it by the look of them."

Private Elcombe was the only one in earshot and seemed perfectly at home behind the wheel. He piped up, "I'm happy. Means I can collect on a bet I've got with my brother as to who's going to get back to England first. Got a tanner resting on it."

Now that they were away from Dieppe, the comment brought both Stock and Dunn back to the reality that life was still going on as normal elsewhere; especially as the bet was for such a small sum as a sixpence.

"How long do you think?" Stock enquired.

"If it stays like this, I'd say six or seven hours. She's handling quite well and there's no swell to speak of." He looked up and around at the sky. "Not much good for fishing though. Not enough wind to drive the waves, unless you're deep line fishing."

Stock spotted a bench towards the back of the boat next to Day and decided he could do with it. "Let me know if you see anything."

"No point in posting lookouts, is there, sir? I mean, we haven't got anything to defend ourselves with anyway." Day looked quite comfortable propped against the side. "What are we going to do when we get back?"

Stock hadn't had a chance to think about this. They would have to report to the port command post in any case, wherever that may be, depending upon where they landed. Somehow he would try to make contact with that Admiral - what was his name? - Godfrey and tell him about Rutherford. He checked his pockets to see if he still had the crystal and piece of paper he had retrieved from the briefcase and found that he had two pieces of folded paper. As Day watched him, he looked at them in the vain hope of finding out a little more, but it was mostly mathematical formulae which he didn't understand.

"These are from Rutherford's briefcase. He was trying to get them back to Portsmouth. Probably best if you don't know more than that, but we'll need to find an Admiral Godfrey, so we'll report to command first and ask them," he said.

"If we get back to England," Day replied. H was curious but decided not to ask further as the boat suddenly lurched more than it had already been doing so.

"Keep half an eye out, will you. I'm going to catch up on sleep," Stock returned, and lay down full stretch on the bench, jamming his body at an angle so that the roll of the boat would not throw him onto the deck. Before he drifted off, he mused that so far he had not had much of an illustrious military career. He was trying to weigh up what he had constructed against what he had destroyed since leaving the officer training camp and decided that a very uneven set of scales was set against him. Back on the farm, his father had told him that a man could be measured by what he had created in life and to always be constructive. He had personally rebuilt several of the aging barns and had been halfway through erecting a new and much bigger farmhouse when war had broken out. After reaching a finishing point, he had volunteered for the Royal Engineers and had enjoyed several months at Deptford depot learning how to construct everything, military style. He was not a youngster, but the passage of time did not allow him to be promoted to first Lieutenant so he would have to wait until he had spent time in the field. The four hangars and a block of latrines at Frévent was all he could put down to his credit and on the other side was the complete destruction of an airfield along with thousands of gallons of valuable petrol. He hoped he would get the chance to even the scales and dreamed of building a new airfield, bigger, longer, busier with lots of planes coming and going, even at night. A smooth runway without any mole hills that would not rock a crew to and fro… to and fro… to and fro.

"Sir! Sir!" It was Day rocking him gently awake, not the aircraft he had been in a moment ago. "England, sir!"

It was almost dark, but he could make the outline of a town. "Elcombe thinks it might be Beachy Head and Eastbourne just beyond."

Stock's body complained as he got up and went over to have a word with Elcombe in the wheelhouse. "Have we got any navigation lights?"

"Not sure, let's have a look. Got a few switches here but it doesn't say what they do, and even if it did, I can't read French anyway. Do you want me to find out?"

"Probably better that they see us clearly rather than firing a shot at us, so yes, try one."

The first didn't do anything that was obvious, but when Elcombe twisted another, a string of small white lights over one of the hoops across the back that they had not noticed earlier, came on. He twisted another and the glow of red and green either side of the wheelhouse shone out into the night.

"Can't miss us now, sir. Do you want me to aim for the town or the port?"

Less than an hour later they passed the harbour wall and were beckoned to an empty berth by a platoon officer waiting for them with a squad of soldiers. It took over an hour before a lorry with a red cross on the side arrived to take the injured away, but those who could walk were escorted away to a billet. On Stock's insistence, he kept Day with him as they were accompanied by a lieutenant to a separate billet in the town which indeed turned out to be Eastbourne and were given directions as to where to report to in the morning.

Day had been up and about earlier than Stock and had managed to purloin a bar of soap and a shaving kit, together with mugs of tea for them. He was also armed with stories of a massive evacuation from Dunkirk. From his account it seemed that most of the evacuees were being taken to either Dover or Folkestone. Since Eastbourne was another thirty miles or so further down the coast, only two other boats had made it as far as they had during the night. In the mess hut, they were each given a bowl of hot porridge from a makeshift canteen, and they joined a group of soldiers on one of the long benches, spooning the mushy breakfast. There were no tables.

"Just wanted to thank you, sir, for getting us out," said a voice. Sergeant Dunn had appeared out of nowhere in front of Stock. "Wouldn't be here if it wasn't for you, and the lads asked me to pass on their thanks." He motioned towards the far side where Stock recognised some of the faces from the previous day. They were mostly smiling and looking at him. One waved. He felt embarrassed but acknowledged them with a nod. "Anytime you need a hand kidnapping another boat, just let me know, sir," Dunn added with a grin.

Before Stock could respond, a smartly dressed sergeant appeared in the open end of the hut and started shouting out orders as to who was to go where and when. The varying groups of soldiers started to shuffle out of the building. Stock and Day were among the last to leave and they turned in a different direction to the others, Day keeping step and a little behind in military fashion. Waiting in an outer office along with several others, mainly more senior officers who looked down their noses at their very shabby uniforms, it wasn't until nearly midday when they were called. Stock had been musing over the unwritten army adage: 'Hurry up and wait.' The major behind the wide desk noted their details and was about to issue them with written orders as to where to go when Stock told Day to wait outside.

Once alone with the major, he told him about Rutherford and showed him the two pieces of paper but left the crystal in his pocket and didn't reveal what it might be used for. The name of Admiral Godfrey had the desired effect and the major picked up the telephone. Several calls and some twenty minutes later, Stock had fresh orders in his hand, directing him and Day to Portsmouth immediately. Regardless of where they were going, they would need new uniforms and at the NAAFI stores, they were provided with incomplete and ill-fitting outfits.

The train journey that followed the south coast took them the rest of the day and it wasn't until dark that they arrived at their designated hotel, The Keppel's Head. Stock was surprised to learn that two rooms had already been reserved for them, along with a most welcome meal of ham and eggs. With a chuckle, the governor proclaimed that he was well used to navy types coming and going at all hours but that they should ignore the ghost that had a tendency to knock on doors in the small hours. Ghosts and the like were the last thing on their minds as they both enjoyed the most comfortable beds they had slept in for weeks.

Their orders stated that they were to report to HMS Sultan at 08.00 hours but when Stock asked one of the waiters for directions he received another surprise.

"That'll be HMS Sultan up on the old military road then, not down by the docks," he replied. Seeing the quizzical look on their faces, he continued. "It's not a ship, it's a land base about, oh, half a mile up the hill on the other side of the river. Nowhere near the sea. You'd best get a move on if you want to be there by eight. The ferry leaves in half an hour and it's a good twenty minutes' walk on from there." He glanced at the grandfather clock in the corner.

They made it without getting lost and were escorted straight away from the guard post at the entrance to a surprisingly imposing building, set among rows of brick-built warehouses. They waited in a carpeted room without any seats and only one small window on the second floor, while their escort stood 'at ease' by the door; it wasn't clear to Stock if he was guarding them or the building. There was a civilian dressed in a worn sporting jacket propping himself against the corner and twiddling his thumbs, but other than a brief look, he ignored them. Confirmation of it being eight o'clock was endorsed by a striking clock in the background but before the last chime struck, a Wren appeared from behind the other door and ushered them into a much larger office where an officer was shuffling papers behind his desk and another attending to a filing cabinet. She continued past other empty desks, knocked on a door set in the far wall and stood to one side allowing Stock and Day through it. Then she closed it behind them without saying a word.

Rear Admiral Godfrey had his eyes shut. He was sitting comfortably back with his hands clasped over his stomach in a voluminous armchair behind an imposing desk centred in the carpeted room, which looked more like a lounge rather than an office. A bookshelf lined one wall half-filled with books and figurines opposite open windows which spanned the other side of the room. Behind him and within arm's reach was another large desk not quite cluttered with files, in-trays and two telephones. All in all, it exuded a place of calm only interrupted by the ticking of a wooden bracket clock mounted above the fireplace.

Standing directly in front of the desk, Stock and Day saluted smartly. The latter was waiting for his officer to make the introductions. Both men had started to wonder whether the admiral was in fact asleep as there was no sign of any movement. Stock decided he had to say something, so he started to say, "Second Lieutenant St…" but Godfrey's right hand went up immediately to silence him.

"I know who you are." The eyes opened to reveal their brown colour. "Yes, you do look like you've had a bit of a rough time of it. Have a seat."

They pulled up a matching pair of half round chairs from against the wall behind them.

"In case you don't know, I'm Rear Admiral Godfrey and, until further notice, your commanding officer. Your unit back at base has been informed so don't worry about having to report there." His voice was smooth but with an edge and it emanated from a mouth that didn't seem to move very much. "I'd like you to tell me - both of you, that is - everything that happened in France and in particular anything to do with Rutherford, but please don't be tempted to embellish your story with acts of heroism etcetera. I can get that down the dockyard."

Naturally, it was Stock who recounted their tale, but it felt like it had all happened an age ago and from time to time, Day prompted him with his perspective. All the while, Godfrey scribbled notes on a piece of paper in front of him, but they couldn't tell what from their viewpoint. When it came to the part where they were describing Rutherford's burial, Stock produced the two sheets of paper and the crystal and put them on the desk. Godfrey held his hand up, leaned forward and retrieved the crystal, which he inspected closely before replacing it carefully.

"Continue."

"Corporal Day isn't aware of what Rutherford told me in the barn. Perhaps it might be prudent if he didn't know," Stock suggested as looked over at Day. "Sorry."

"That's ok, sir. I probably wouldn't understand it anyway," Day reassured him.

"Leave that bit out for the moment. Carry on!" Godfrey motioned at Stock with his pencil.

Their story petered out towards the end and Godfrey called a halt to it, sat back and closed his eyes again, tapping his fingers in an arch as his elbows rested on the arms of the chair. It was as though he was judging their statement and deciding what length of sentence to hand out.

"You're quite a brave and resourceful man, aren't you, Lieutenant?" he asked as he opened his eyes again. "And you, Corporal, have done your duty by supporting him. Well done. Both of you."

Stock was embarrassed by the compliments and hoped it didn't show, but he didn't say anything as Godfrey maintained the silence for a short while.

"Anything more to add, Corporal?"

"No, sir, other than I wouldn't be here but for the lieutenant."

"Thank you, Corporal. Wait outside."

Once the door was closed, Godfrey leaned forward and looked closely at the disfigured pieces of paper. "Now, tell me what Rutherford said, word for word if you can."

It was an impossible task, but he recounted as much as he could remember, and it dawned on him that this really was as important as Rutherford had made out; his mere presence in front of an admiral emphasised that.

"Do you know anything about the workings of the modern wireless?"

"Not much, sir, other than they use valves and need electricity to work. I've had our set at home apart a few times trying to get better reception. Turned out to be a loose aerial connection."

"Then you won't know anything about radar, then?"

"I understand that it works on the same principle but that's about all."

"And you certainly won't know anything about underwater radar either?"

"Only what Rutherford told me, but I wouldn't know how to go about what he does."

Godfrey mulled over Stock's answers and motioned to the artefacts Stock had put on his desk. "I'm in a bit of a quandary. What we have here is top secret. Going by the book, you should be court marshalled just for knowing about Rutherford. If it came to that, there are those who might claim you coerced Rutherford into going with you, exposed him to danger so much so that it cost him his life, stole his case and returned to England so that you could either sell it back to us or to some other party. In a matter as serious as this I would think the prosecution would call for imprisonment, at least until the war is over. On the other hand, you have done exactly the right thing by returning this to me and certainly by keeping this out of German hands. I owe you something for that at least."

Stock was appalled, as Godfrey had intended him to be. He had never considered anything to do with Court Marshalls and certainly not in association with his recent actions, but there was a real threat there and he suspected this admiral probably had the power to ensure that it was carried out. Not only would his military career be finished, but the stigma in civilian life would follow him like a ball and chain; even his family would spurn him.

Once his initial shock subsided, he realised that he was being presented with two options and that what he said next would determine whether he went to prison or remained in the army. He found himself wringing his hands, thankfully just below the level of the desk and out of sight, stopped, placed them firmly on his knees, and returned Godfrey's stern stare. Those steady brown eyes seemed to pierce his thoughts and he felt sure that Godfrey didn't just want him to protest his innocence. That would be a crass thing to do. That is what the average man would do. That was not what he was going to do, and he searched for an alternative that would rescue him.

"What about the buried case in France. If that could somehow be retrieved, would that help?"

Godfrey held his stare for several moments and Stock knew he was out of the woods when a widening smile split the seriousness of his face. "I was hoping you would say something like that. I pride myself in being a pretty good judge of character and so far you haven't disappointed me." He leaned round and lifted one of the telephones. "Ask Mr. Morris to come in."

Stock noted that he was not giving him his approval, just that he was not disapproving.

The Wren opened the door for Mr. Morris who turned out to be the man in civvies Stock had seen earlier. He wasn't twiddling his thumbs, but his fingers played with each other, and he came and sat down next to Stock without looking at him.

"Have a look at these, will you, and tell me what you think," Godfrey drawled, pointing to the papers on his desk and the crystal that acted as their paperweight.

Stock and Godfrey waited while Mr. Morris played with the crystal before examining the papers. "Is this it? Is this all there is?"

"For the time being, yes. What do you make of it?"

"I… I really can't tell, but it looks real enough, and it has the same sheen that Rutherford described." He peered more closely at the crystal. "I'd have to put it through our spectrometer in the lab to be sure."

"What about the formula?"

He fiddled with the papers. "There's not much here of any use. A lot of the ink's run and it still doesn't tell us where it came from." He looked up at Godfrey. "There is more, isn't there?"

"That's all you've got to work with at the moment. So please trot along to your lab and let me know the minute you have something."

Mr. Morris just sat there looking between the papers and the crystal. Godfrey brought him out of his oblivion.

"Now please, Mr. Morris."

"Of course. Straight away. By lunchtime, maybe." Mr. Morris stood up and left.

Godfrey opened a file on his desk. "Tell me if I leave anything out. Now, let's have a look. Born 24th April 1910, one of two sons. Two sisters. Father an officer in the 17th Lancers, grandfather an officer in the same amalgamated regiment. Occupation stated as farmer and builder. Volunteered October 1939, officer training corps at Deptford and Chatham, commissioned into the Royal Engineers in March, sponsored by Colonel Alfredson. It says here you enjoy skiing, rugby, tennis, golf, cricket and that you are quite a useful Bridge player. Bit of an all-rounder, eh? Which rugby team did you play for?"

"Wing-forward for Ely, sir, and no, you haven't left anything out so far but perhaps you ought to add mobile target for the Luftwaffe." Stock wondered if he had overstepped the mark, but he felt that it wouldn't hurt to find out just what sort of a man his new commander was.

Godfrey jerked his head up from the file at Stock's last comment. "I'll also have to add a sense of humour won't I? Skiing's a bit unusual….where do you go for that?"

"Jean and I, my sister, spent three weeks in Kitzbuhel a couple of years ago and a wonderful place it is too. Came across some chaps from the British army ski team who were training there, and it made me realise how relatively unfit I was, but we skied the Hahnenkamm every day and in the end I was showing them up. We woke one morning to find that overnight the Germans had annexed the entire country. One day the Austrian flags were flying, the next they had been replaced with much bigger Nazi ones, draped all over the place. We even shook hands with Von Ribbentrop once when he came over. Smarmy sort of fellow and Jean took an instant disliking to the man when he started eyeing her up."

"Anything useful I ought to know about him?"

"Not really. He was there on a bit of a holiday I think. He arrived soon after some of the Alpenkorps and I think it was more of a publicity exercise as there was an army of photographers with him. He made an address to them in the snow and all us foreigners had to line up while he did so. Must have been a good speaker though as even the locals were cheering at the end, but we didn't understand a word and we didn't join in. He left two days later."

"Umm. What sort of Bridge do you play?"

There were several answers to this question and Stock realised he was being probed, not so that Godfrey would be able to assess his skill at Bridge but to obtain a greater knowledge of the workings of his mind and if he really was made of the right material. His background was steady enough and he had proved his patriotism, yet he was being asked for more, specifically to establish if he was more than just capable of applying himself only when the need arose. That he could rise above a situation and take control was similar to playing Bridge, which had once been described to him as 'the art of making the best from a bad hand.' He decided to play the game with Godfrey and return the probe.

"I think four No Trump is a good starting point," he referred to Blackwood's Convention, which required his partner to respond. He was asking Godfrey to let him know if he was able to support his aggressive slam invitation.

Godfrey's eyes narrowed a little as he considered the challenge and recognised the parry. "If you're going down that route, I'd like to be able to reply with something stronger, but I don't hold all the aces which is why you're here." The response told Stock that this was a pragmatic man who understood him.

He looked down at the folder again. "I see you're not married. Any reason?"

"None in particular other than I enjoy a bachelors' life. In case you're wondering, no, I am not homosexual."

"I think you might fit in nicely." Godfrey closed the folder indicating that he was satisfied. "Do you think you could find Rutherford's case again easily?"

The change of tack caught him out and he had to think about it. "I don't see why not. Apart from being able to get there and back and a few Germans that are bound to be strutting about I'm sure I could locate it again." He suddenly understood what was going to be asked of him and exactly why he was here. One of the many pieces of advice he had received from his father just before he had left for the OTC came to mind. 'Always volunteer. Don't wait to be volunteered.'

"If you can arrange the transport, I can get it back for you."

"You're quick, aren't you? I hope that's not going to be necessary, but I fear Morris will tell me he needs what's in that case."

A satisfying glow ran through Stock at Godfrey's compliment; it had been a long time since anyone of merit had complimented him.

Godfrey continued, "The prime minister called me into see him barely two weeks ago and told me in no uncertain terms that we had to do something very quickly about the U-boats. Just last month we lost over 100,000 tons of shipping and it's getting worse and if we can't keep that lifeline from America open then we'll be strangled into submission. Starved even.

"Morris and his team have been working on extending the range of our ASDIC machines, an underwater sonar that actively seeks submarines rather than relying upon hydrophones that only listen. Those crystals in Rutherford's case are made from a special type of quartz and are somehow able to increase the radio band width to very high frequency, known as VHF for short. And they tell me this will enable their sets to locate those U-boats up to a couple of miles away, maybe more. They are even working on other forms of quartz that will produce ultra-high frequency, but right now we need to concentrate on what we've got. Or rather what you're going to get. I can't tell you what other plans we have to deal with the shipping losses, only that we are relying on those crystals. Perhaps you can see now just how important this is but remember, this comes under the new official secrets act, so don't go telling anyone else about this."

He stood up and took a few paces to over to the window. his back to Stock. "The fear of submarine attack makes one shudder, especially when you know you're the target. You don't sleep well at night and every noise out of the ordinary wakes you. Consequentially, you're not as alert the next day and it's all too easy to make a bad decision. Your appetite disappears and you develop a nervousness where one didn't exist before and you get to hate the hidden enemy. I've seen what a torpedo attack can do to a perfectly normal person. If they're lucky enough to survive, they're not the same afterwards. The difference between life or death doesn't seem to rest upon your decision as to what ship or whom to send into a certain situation, but rather it's more like the roll of a dice. In this instance I'd like to make sure that that dice is loaded in our favour. You can see what I'm getting at, can't you?"

He spun round to stare at Stock who didn't respond to the rhetorical question.

"I'm sending you into that same position where the enemy is unseen at the moment, below the surface if you like, but you mustn't let that affect you. You aren't showing any signs of shell shock even though it sounds like you had a bit of a tough time of it over in France. In some instances, there's a delayed response to being shot at and, in your case, nearly blown up as well, but you seem more than alright to me." He paused to allow Stock to reflect. "It is vital we retrieve that case."

Stock got the impression that Godfrey wouldn't normally have revealed his own fears to just anybody but by doing so to him, it added to the weight attached to what he was being asked to do. Right now, that made him important and at least he had been given a reason why which was most unusual in the military.

"I'll do my best, sir," he muttered. It was all he could manage.

Godfrey returned to his chair. "It's going to take a couple of days or so to put things together, figure how we get you there and back etcetera but leave that to me. You may as well take it easy until then but stay at The Keppel where I can reach you and if you're asked why or what you're doing, don't mention me or this department and say that you've been told to look into rock samples or something like that. As an Engineer that'll be believable. On another matter, you've displayed all the right attributes that go with command so I'm having you promoted to captain with immediate effect. When you leave here make sure you get a more suitable uniform. My secretary will draw up your papers so wait in the outer office while she does that."

The stunning news was so unexpected that Stock couldn't think of any smart retort other than, "Thank you, sir." By all rights, he would have expected to be promoted to first lieutenant in a few months and then have to wait another year or so before receiving his captaincy. He stood, saluted, and was about to turn and leave when another thought came to him. "What about Corporal Day? He's a good man to have around and if I have trouble finding the case then he may be able to help."

"You're quite right. I'll consider it. Good morning, Captain. Ask her to come in, would you?"

Chapter 7
Pompey

Over a rationed lunch in The Keppel's Head restaurant, Stock reflected that the Wren couldn't have been more helpful by providing them with all the necessary paperwork and a roughly sketched map of Portsmouth and Southsea. Being separated from their unit it would otherwise have been very awkward, but the admiral's signature on the requisition chit worked like a magic wand and they had authority to draw pay and equipment from the quartermaster general, as well as updated travel permits billeting them at the same hotel. Stock was told to return the following morning to collect his new uniform.

"She said there was a show on at The King's Theatre in Southsea and she's even marked it on the map here. Why don't we go and have a look? I can't remember what she said it was called, but I'm sure the barman will know." Day seemed to have boundless energy and was half-way through his second pint which was lasting just a little longer than the first. "It starts in a couple of hours and it's only a short walk."

Stock wanted to write some letters to his family and catch up with the newspapers as well as some more sleep, so allowed Day to go off on his own. It had been an extraordinary few days and he felt he needed time to digest all that had happened to him and what might happen to him in the near future. There was only one other civilian was in the lounge where he sat and wrote to his family, mindful of Godfrey's warning about keeping things to himself, when a lieutenant-commander and his coxswain came and sat down opposite. With them came the strong smell of the sea. It wasn't a big room and despite their efforts to keep their conversation to themselves, Stock understood that they had been ferrying troops from Dunkirk to Dover for the past few days and were docked for repairs. 'Must be from one of destroyers' he thought.

The next morning, as good as the quartermaster's word, his new uniform was ready on time and fitted well in most places. Even his boots were comfortable but could do with some breaking in. He was sitting in his room polishing them. Now that he had a bit of time to himself, he mulled over the past few days and dwelt on the early morning attack outside Oisemont. The speed they had traversed the countryside on their BSAs meant that the Germans would have had to continue through the night to catch up with them. Perhaps that had been their general orders. Although he wasn't trained in military manoeuvres, he thought it unwise for any army to cross into enemy held territory in the pitch black of night. Perhaps they had been elements of another unit, or even a bigger corps, but for whatever reason someone in the enemy camp had had them in their sights that early in the morning.

His thoughts were interrupted when the landlord knocked on his door and handed him a sealed envelope. There was one small plain piece of paper within. It had the words 'Report to Room P at 16.30' written on it and was signed with the letter 'G.'

This time at the security barrier outside HMS Sultan, instead of being escorted they were directed to one of the warehouses. Entering through a side door, were confronted with two other doors marked 'Room P' and 'Room Q.' The dividing wall merely split the building into two parts, 'P' being much smaller. Dressed in his new, clean uniform, Stock felt rather proud as he led the way to the table where two men were sitting with their backs to them. He drew up a chair on the far side. Day copied him.

"Weren't you a lieutenant yesterday?"

He looked across the table to see the same lieutenant-commander from The Keppel's Head. Having had a good night's sleep, he was feeling much more like himself again and able to retort straight away. "And I see you're still just a lieutenant-commander. You should have joined the army, not the navy."

It was a cheeky reply, but he felt emboldened by his promotion. Not that Stock had come across the issue before, but it was a well discussed point about who out ranked whom in the three armed services. In this instance, a naval lieutenant-commander was about the equivalent of an army captain or a major and a squadron leader in the royal air force, but the differences were a bit of a grey area when it came to seniority and on whose territory one was.

His reply brought a smile to the lieutenant-commander's face. He introduced himself, "Robin Ruddock. This is my coxswain, John Roberts."

"From one of the destroyers? I overheard you talking yesterday."

"Er, no, not quite. I think we'd best leave it up to the admiral to explain."

"This is George Day and a very handy chap too," Stock added. Day's rank was evident from the chevrons on his sleeve.

While they were talking, Stock observed the lieutenant-commander whose craggy face said it all. Presumably, he had been born with unnaturally bushy eyebrows and hadn't grown them especially to protect his eyes from salty winds of the sea. The excess nasal hair protruding from his pointed nose and small blood vessels surfaced evenly on each cheek indicated he had spent plenty of time on an open bridge. Stock looked down at the scratched surface of his watch to see just how long he would have to wait to find out more about Ruddock when another door opened at the far end of the building. Admiral Godfrey and another man were preceded by the Wren who seated herself on his right at the table.

"Good morning, gentlemen. I presume you have introduced yourselves. This is Lieutenant Peter Brown and he'll be joining you on this expedition as your arms expert." He indicated the man who sat next to the Wren, and Stock saw the dark-haired younger man meet their gazes in turn. "The long and the short of it is that I've had to put this together in a bit of a hurry as time is very much against us. The longer we wait, the better prepared the enemy will be and at the moment he doesn't know we're coming but it's got every chance of success if we move quickly before he prepares his defence. It's a simple plan and I'm afraid that only Captain Stock and his corporal will have the full picture. Only those of us seated round this table know anything about this, so let's keep it that way."

While he was speaking, the Wren unfolded a large map and a naval chart and placed them in the centre of the table.

The Admiral continued, "So that you all know, it's Captain Stock's job together with the corporal and Mr. Brown's, to retrieve a briefcase from outside a village called Oisemont in northern France and it's Ruddock's job to ferry them there and back. From the reports we've been receiving from some of the evacuees, it seems that the Germans have not yet crossed the Varenne, that's the river that runs through Dieppe, but are concentrating on their encirclement of Calais and Dunkirk. I'm told that the evacuation from there is only going to continue for another couple of days and while it is, we ought to be able to use that as cover for our operation. Fortunately, the weather's on our side for a change, as the Met Office reports that there'll be low cloud for at least the next twenty-four hours or so and that means no enemy aircraft. After that, the wind's supposed to change direction and bring a bit of a storm so we have to make the most of it now while we can.

The Wren had placed what looked like a small wooden chess pawn on the village of Oisemont.

"From what you've been told, and what you know about that part of the coast, where do you think you can land our party?"

Godfrey was looking for Ruddock's response and he now leaned over both maps for a closer look. "I'd go due south out of Portsmouth to about mid-channel, turn to port and cut across to where we see the coast then turn north-east and follow it to about this point. I wouldn't want to go too much further than Eu as there's a large sandbar that stretches from about there all the way up to where the Somme meets the Channel at Le Crotoy. The draught's minimal but it would need to be at high tide since it goes out a very long way at low. I think there's a jetty just about here, north of Ault.

That's about as close as I could get and that leaves, oh, about fifteen miles or so to Oisemont." He straightened up. "I'd have to look at my tables to confirm but high tide'll probably be about midnight or soon after."

"Um… I agree. The more you keep to the west before spotting the French coast, the better," Godfrey addressed those on his right. "Mr. Ruddock has had years of experience in the Channel. He's based in Jersey and knows where the minefields are which is why I've asked him to be your chaperone. Getting you there's the easy part. Now to you three gentlemen. We can't send you in by plane because of the weather and I don't like putting all my eggs in one basket just in case you get shot down. Besides which, the three of you plus the pilot would mean a bigger plane which may or may not be able to land in the given space, especially at night. We've already tried that and failed. I can't expect you to walk fifteen miles across France and back again in the few hours of darkness, so I've taken a leaf out of your book.

He was looking at Stock.

"We're going to strap three motorcycles to the side of Ruddock's boat. An MTB. It's got a shallow enough draft as Ruddock here pointed out, it's capable of over forty knots and has plenty of armament."

'Here we go again, back into the Channel,' thought Stock, but he had to admit a motor torpedo boat at forty knots would probably make the crossing in a tenth of the time it had taken just two days ago.

Godfrey looked over at Ruddock and took up the discourse, "I've already checked the tide timetables and you're right. High tide is just after midnight and advances about twenty minutes per day. I want you to leave at 20.00 hours Zulu to make sure you catch it. Once you drop them off, I suggest you stand off some miles and come in again just before dawn; we don't want any inquisitive Jerries taking pot shots at you. You can arrange a time and a torch signal with Stock's party. I know it will be getting on for low tide then, but they won't be encumbered with the bikes and if it comes to it, they can wade out to you." He turned to Stock. "Don't forget to keep the contents of that case dry."

He turned back to Ruddock to add, "If they can't make that rendezvous with you, I don't want you exposed more than you have to be during daylight hours, so you'll return here without them. For the following two nights, you're to go back to the same jetty at midnight. Clear?"

"What if we can't make that jetty?"

"Then you'll just have to improvise. Take a couple of ramps and some extra rope." Godfrey's tone indicated that Ruddock ought not to let something as trivial as a jetty get in the way of his plans.

He now focused on Stock, asking, "You've driven those roads, how long do you think it'll take you to get there, dig up the case and get back? Let's assume for the minute there's no Germans."

It was Stock's turn to lean over the table. He studied the familiar map and was pleased to see that he and Day had already driven the last part of the route, but the first part would be new to them. He knew how confusing the roads were in the French towns and villages and how easy it was to get lost but it looked straight forward enough. "Once we clear Ault it should take less than an hour then, say, about ten minutes to locate the case and another hour to return. All in all, just over two hours but if Mr. Ruddock gets us to the jetty at midnight, we ought to allow half an hour to unload the bikes, half an hour for getting lost in the dark and another half an hour to find the jetty again, so that'll bring it to 03.30. Sunrise must be about 05.30 at the moment and it starts to get light about an hour before that, so to be on the safe side we ought to be ready for pick up from 03.30 onwards." He paused to let the outcome of his logical verdict sink in. "But when we left Oisemont, we saw troop-= carriers racing for the coast and we have to assume that it was either field artillery or at least one other tank that took out the Matilda, so there will be Germans in the area, therefore we ought to add on yet another half an hour for diverting around them. I'd be happy at making the rendezvous at 04.00 Zulu."

The others had all been looking at Stock while he laid out the timetable and none of them could fault it, but it was now over to Godfrey for approval.

"I like your assessment, but I think you will find that those Germans you saw were probably heading for Dieppe and will no longer be in Oisemont as it doesn't appear to have any military value. But there may well be others joining them, so I've come up the idea of getting you to wear German helmets." He waited a few seconds to see if any of the assembly could work out why. "It will be almost impossible for anyone to recognise you at night at all except for your heads which will show up in any headlamps. If you get caught, you can discard them quickly enough.

Nobody asked where the helmets were coming from. "Now, any questions?.......Good. You've got three hours before you leave, and you can collect your equipment from Room Q next door. Good luck, gentlemen."

Godfrey and the Wren remained seated while the others filed out.

"Er, Stock, just one more thing," he called out and waited until Stock came within easy talking distance. "When you come back with the case, make sure you bring it straight to me at my office and don't let the others see what's in it."

Chapter 8

Deer

He could see now why Ruddock's face looked the way it did by the way the cold stinging spray arched over the bows as if its only target was the men gathered in the rear. It hadn't taken Stock and his party long to seek the shelter of the small cabin below the open wheelhouse. Before he ducked down into the comparative shelter he looked up at the coxswain manning the wheel along with another sailor, both acting as though this were a Sunday pleasure cruise while the lookout behind him - who doubled up as a machine gunner - was leaning against the safety rail as if he was in his local. Stock was glad to see that, despite this nonchalant pose, he was simultaneously scanning the sea and the skies.

"We drink cocoa on this boat, but not when we're going twenty-five knots." Ruddock grinned and looked at them unsuccessfully for a reaction. "Might light the stove when we get nearer the coast if we have time, but meanwhile can I suggest you relax a little. There's nothing out here that can catch us, not even the latest E-boats, and we've still got another hour before we have to think about reducing speed." He indicated to the padded benches that ran alongside the cabin and, once they were seated, unhinged a tabletop from one end and propped it up with a wooden pole that clipped into place at the other.

It was Lieutenant Brown who broke the relative silence over the drone of the powerful engines and occasional thump from a sturdy wave on the bows. "I suppose the admiral has a lot of faith in you. I mean, bringing you all the way from Jersey just to ferry us about."

"Oh, we haven't come from Jersey, we're only based there. We've been pulled off evacuation duty between Dover and Dunkirk just to make sure you don't get your feet wet. I feel so sorry for those poor sods who are going to be stranded and there's still thousands of them to get out. Because of our shallow draft we could moor against the smaller piers and were taking mostly wounded but I've lost count of the number of times we went to and fro. I lost two ratings in a Stuka machine gun attack while we were there, but he must have run out of shells because if he'd carried on down the boat, he'd have taken most of the rest of us as well; you saw the repaired damage as you got on."

From the quayside they had been watching the crew wheel the three BSAs up a ramp and onto the deck of the MTB where they were lashed to the torpedo launchers. At the same time, the lookout railings were being replaced by one of the dockyard team, but they hadn't attempted to cover up the several the bullet holes.

"It makes me wonder what's so important that you fellows want to go back to France when the rest of the army is going in the opposite direction," he chuckled ironically almost as if to sneer at them.

Stock had wondered when Ruddock would raise this question and had already decided not to fob him off by quoting something from the official secrets act but to ingratiate him by telling him something akin to the truth. After all, this was the man who would be risking his life and his crew as well as his boat to make sure they all got back to England, and they might need him to stick his neck out a little more than he would do otherwise. He waited, feigning indecision. until Peter Brown answered, "Sorry, can't tell you. Under admiral's orders."

"I can tell you." Brown's head whipped round to stare at Stock who met it with a look that matched, and at that point his suspicions were confirmed that Brown was Godfrey's man and sent by him to keep more than just an eye on them. He didn't know just how much Brown had been told by Godfrey and he hoped his ploy would smoke him out as he couldn't very well just ask him when they were probably both under the same strict orders not to tell anyone. He held up his hand at Brown but addressed Ruddock, "I've been told it's all about steel and a new kind of ore that produces a stronger alloy. The case we had to leave behind contains certain items and apparently they're very important to the boffins. We had to leave it behind because a regiment of Germans was on top of us at the time, but the admiral was quite insistent that we had to retrieve it, and pronto."

"I don't think Mr. Ruddock needed to know that and I shall have to let the admiral know that you've divulged information you were specifically told not to. Under the circumst…"

Stock took the opportunity to put Brown in his place and rounded on him. "Under the circumstances I've taken the decision to let Mr. Ruddock know why he's been called away from what is obviously one very important job to another very important job and while we all follow orders and would like to know why, we rarely get told. If he and his crew are going to be bobbing around in the middle of the Channel like sitting ducks, I'd like to give him a reason why he shouldn't take off at the earliest opportunity and leave us behind. What we've been charged with here is returning that case to Admiral Godfrey in good order and if that means letting Mr. Ruddock know he has to wait around longer for us with enemy aircraft trying to blow his guts out of the water, then I'd say that qualifies as a necessity. He knows about the case and some of the crew will see it when we return anyway so what I've told him he'd see for himself. Furthermore, the admiral hasn't told you everything and as I'm the only one here who does know what's going on, if I deem it necessary to divulge something to a trusted officer, then it's my decision and not yours. In future keep your comments to yourself and concentrate on your job which is primarily to get that case back to the admiral if we don't."

While it was a big put down in front of others and was clearly designed to establish Stock as the legitimate leader, it was also to let

Brown know that Stock knew a lot more about him than he thought. Brown opened his mouth to retort and then thought the better of it and lowered his eyes to avert Stock's stare; the worm of uncertainty had done its job.

He turned to Ruddock and added, "I'm sorry to have had to talk about you in your presence but both time and space are at a bit of a premium round here." In the cramped cabin Ruddock had been taken back a little by the harangue and Day would have disappeared under the bench if he could have. "You see, I've got to ask you to give us some latitude here because I suspect our timetable is likely to be disrupted by a very active enemy. What Corporal Day and I experienced only two days ago was that the Germans chasing us knew exactly what they were doing and were after that briefcase for themselves. They don't know we haven't got it yet and they'll probably be scouring the area for it, hopefully in Dieppe and not Oisemont. So, while the admiral's principle of surprise is correct, I think you're going to have to be very much on your toes when we get close to the coast and I'm asking if you can be as ready as you can with your rubber life raft in the morning and wait as long as you can."

They all knew Stock was asking Ruddock to go against the admiral's direct orders to return to Portsmouth if they didn't show by 04.00 and the grimace on his face displayed his anxiety. Stock noted that Brown stayed silent.

"My hands are tied but I can cross slowly in front of Ault for a few minutes on the way home if that helps. Say another fifteen minutes?" Ruddock replied, reluctantly.

"I'm not sure I heard the admiral state exactly what time you had to leave, only that you were not to expose yourself during daylight hours. If the cloud is going to be as low as predicted, then it'll be darker for longer."

"We'll see. I'll give you as long as I can but in any case, we'll need to be on our way by 04.30."

"Fair enough." Stock relaxed a little. "Now I'd like to go over our route and memorise as much as we can. You've got the map, Corporal."

Day spread it out on the table and Ruddock retreated to the relatively uncomplicated task of commanding an MTB from the upper deck. Stock wanted them to stay on the minor roads. Once away from Ault, there was one that would suit although there were several complicated junctions including the N28 that they would have to cross anyway. Without the sun or any stars to assist, and with hooded headlamps as their only illumination, it was going to be tricky, and Stock marked three waypoints where they would stop briefly to ensure they would be on the correct route. He would lead, followed by Brown, with Day in the rear.

"I'd like to bring up the rear," blurted out Brown.

"Why?"

He hesitated just a little, before continuing, "Well….it'll be easier for me to follow the two of you, especially when we get close to Oisemont. After all, you both know where you're going."

Stock considered the request but dismissed the reasoning and asked himself what other motive Brown would have for bringing up the rear, but he couldn't find one. Then another thought occurred to him. "No, I think we'll stick to the order with Day in the rear because if the Jerries were to open fire on us and he and I were next to each other, then there'd more chance of them hitting the both of us. And we're the only two who know exactly where the case is. So. you will be between us."

Brown and Stock stared at each other, but he backed down. "OK, as you say."

While the engines monotonously thrummed and the waves parted, Stock leaned back and closed his eyes in contemplation of what lay ahead, memorising the route, envisaging where they might go wrong and what to do if they came across any Germans. They had all been issued with grenades and Day had been told to keep his rifle while Stock and Brown had been issued with Thompson machine guns in addition to a torch each. Spades had been folded into the panniers of each bike. Now was not the time to reflect upon his actions that had led to a confrontation with Brown, but he wondered if he had been a little foolhardy using his rank for the first time.

The engine notes suddenly reduced to a relative whisper and the boat lurched forward and levelled out as it reduced speed. His watch said 23.30 as Ruddock reappeared down the steps. "Coast's well in sight and we passed Dieppe a few minutes ago so if you want to get up on deck we'll drift in quietly at about 8 knots. Ought to be about 10 minutes or so. By the way, we haven't agreed on a signal yet. I take it you read morse?"

"What have you got in mind?"

"How about US? Nice and simple."

"Ok with me." Stock took the torch from his pocket and practiced 'dot-dot-dash dot-dot-dot' on the wall of the cabin opposite.

"Right then, going dark in one minute."

All ten hands appeared to be on deck and Stock wondered where they had all been during the crossing as he had only seen three of them before. They all peered into the sullen gloom which was only broken by the vague night-time light ahead of them off to starboard. The boat rocked uncomfortably sideways in the windless swell as the burbling engines coaxed their slow progress.

"Jetty two points to starboard, sir." A voice just audible enough to reach the wheel from the bows and the MTB came round a little as the engine note decreased further.

"Swing. Report quarters," Ruddock barked, lowering his binoculars. He was ordering the lead line to assess the depth below their keel to be called out in quarters of a fathom.

The same man tossed the lead weight forwards, singing out, "One and a half." Stock converted the fathom reading to nine feet and although he hadn't asked what the draught of the MTB was, he didn't think it was anywhere near that.

Another minute and a splash. "One and a half."

Even through the dark, they could just see the wooden slatted jetty ahead. "One and a quarter." A little more than seven feet remained beneath them less the keel. Ruddock didn't need to order anything as the bows gently touched the jetty and a rating jumped the narrowing gap to tie off. Others began unstrapping the bikes and releasing the ramps. Stock assumed they had been given their orders earlier in order to minimise noise and he scanned the shoreline for anything that might indicate the presence of the enemy, but there was nothing and without any light he couldn't even see the road he had earlier pictured in his mind. Ruddock had come forward and was overlooking the unloading from the prow and he whipped round when one of the ratings released a ramp with a thud just a little too early and swore.

"23.50. We'll see you in about four hours then. Good luck." From Stock's angle on the jetty, Ruddock's outline with the sky behind him was visible but he realised that Ruddock could hardly see him or the other two and thought he had addressed Brown in the gloom. He went to mount the front BSA but bumped into Brown instead.

"I'll take this one, " Stock stated.

"Why that one?"

"I picked it out when it was being loaded. No other reason."

To get on the right road, Stock knew they would have to go through the village of Ault before turning inland and he was thankful that they had found tarmac rather than impossible shingle as they turned right off the jetty, parallel with the shore. But within half a mile, just after the start of the houses, he stopped, left his engine running as he dismounted, and ripped off the slitted cowling that covered the headlight. He cursed himself for not anticipating that the beam from the headlamp would only illuminate the road directly ahead and effectively blind his night vision to such an extent that he couldn't see where they actually wanted to go. 'Better to see and be seen, than get lost.' Two minutes later he spotted the signpost that he hoped would be there and they turned left onto the narrower road. There was nothing he could do about the noise as it reverberated off the buildings either side in the still night. He had previously told

Brown that he would have to ignore their tell-tale signature. Day already knew.

He mentally ticked off the junctions and kept to a steady speed, stopping very briefly at the first marker point. Nothing else was moving and nobody else was about except them in their own little world that ended at the influence of their headlamps, but Stock knew that somewhere, someone had had their night's sleep disturbed by their passage and prayed that the night would somehow protect them. They rose up one hill into low cloud that enveloped them, but the mist cleared as they entered a wood in the valley, and he brought them to a halt at their second waypoint just before the main road. He looked each way in the distance in case there was anybody coming but again nothing, but he spotted a signpost and even though they were coming from the opposite direction, thought he recognised a small, dilapidated barn from their journey a few days ago.

The next part would be tricky since he had no idea how they had got round Oisemont when they had been outrunning the Germans, but he knew that they had to get to the South side of the town. Now, at a reduced speed, he searched for their third marker but out of nowhere came the first building and before they knew it, they were between walls and houses, hedges and gardens, side roads and gravel tracks. A fork appeared ahead. Despite their German helmets, the last thing Stock wanted to do was to stop in the middle of the town and be seen, so he chose the left. Almost immediately, there was another fork, so he chose to go right in an attempt to even out the odds and find the most direct route. Ahead he could see a 'T' junction and went left, hoping there would be a right soon after, but it kept going left with only lanes between the houses on his right. With a sense of doom, he found he had led them back to just beyond the first fork and he swore in self admonishment that he had taken them in a complete circle. It was too dark to look up and try to find the typical church spire to use as a landmark. This time he chose the alternative road from the fork which immediately dipped and turned and was surrounded by taller buildings indicating that they were nearing the centre. His fears were confirmed when he saw a square ahead, behind which stood an imposing building that he took to be the Town Hall. As they entered the arena, he saw two parallel roads going away from them each side of it and others joining from left and right. 'Like a bloody spider's web' he cursed and chose the right-hand option. That it was the wrong one soon became apparent as the street narrowed round a bend and terminated in a brick wall. They had to make three-point turns, returned to the square and hairpinned right. This time as they approached Stock could see that an inquisitive person had turned on a light on the top floor of one of the terraced houses and was looking out of a window. Frustrated by the tangle of roads, he gunned his engine to get away and followed the wider avenue which mercifully seemed to lead in the direction he hoped was correct. 'Lucky we didn't wake the whole bloody town' he reflected as the buildings spread out and suddenly terminated in open countryside.

They pulled up in about a quarter of a mile and Stock told them to kill their engines and lights and waited while their night vision returned but there was nothing to see other than vague outlines of buildings behind them, let alone recognise anything in the almost pitch dark. This he had anticipated, and he knew he would be faced with the dilemma of either splitting up or remaining together.

"I don't know about anyone else, but I got confused back there. Made a good maze though. I don't think it was this road," volunteered Day.

"Neither do I, but those bloody roads caught me out, and the locals now know someone's here. Look!" They turned to see that a few lights had come on. "We're about the right distance from the town so if we cut across the fields one way or the other, we must come across the burnt-out truck next to the tree sooner or later. I really don't want to do that because of the ditches but the question is, left or right?" He was posing an impossible question to Day, not Brown.

"How about we go further down this road, turn left and left again and come back on ourselves?" Brown offered.

"Why left?"

"Because I'm left-handed and we can't see to toss a coin."

Stock checked the luminous hands on his watch and noted that they were only a few minutes behind schedule. "Ok, we'll do that. Take your light covers off but keep them handy. Move your bike's light to the right and I'll look left."

They kick started their engines and the traversing beams across the fields picked out a number of reflective eyes, mostly rabbits, but there was no sign of their tree. Stock motioned them to move off. He ignored several left turnings as they were dirt tracks and was beginning to wonder just how far they would have to go when they arrived at a crossroads and within a few hundred yards, turned left again. He immediately knew this was not the right road by the way it undulated and meandered between hedges, but he continued anyway, all the while weighing up Brown's idea and praying they wouldn't have to continue searching in a quartering pattern for the rest of the night. Where the tarmac finished at a gravel road on a corner, they turned round, went back and continued along the previous road and soon after, turned left at a 'T' junction. 'This is more like it' thought Stock and he opened the throttle a little more on the flatter road. The minutes ticked by as Stock thought they must be heading for Oisemont, but after too many, he pulled up, u-turned and stopped, facing the others.

"Let's get back to the first crossroads and go straight over, then right." He let out the clutch and moved off with a wheel spin.

Under his breath he was cursing, swearing, damning, and realising that he had boxed them into a corner. Returning to Oisemont was probably the worst option, but then again, so was roaming about the enemy-held French countryside. If only it hadn't been so cloudy. If only there was a little light in the sky. If only they didn't have a rendezvous while it was still dark. If only…

He led them straight at the crossroads, admitting to himself that he ought to have slowed down a little, but he was concentrating on his sense of direction and felt they were being led away from Oisemont by the way the road kept veering to the left. There - a turning to the right at last and he was just applying his brakes when a deer jumped out of nowhere ahead of him. He skidded just a little as his front wheel scrabbled for grip, but he missed it. So did Day, but Brown was less fortunate as a second deer, following the first, broadsided into him and barrelled him and his machine onto the grassy verge. As Stock was turning right, he glanced over his shoulder just in time to see Brown's bike come to a halt with its headlight pointing skywards. He and Day stopped their bikes so that their headlamps illuminated the scene, just as two other deer came bounding across the road on the same path. The one that had knocked Brown off his bike was on its side with its legs pounding the air in a futile effort to get away.

"How many more of those buggers are there?" commented Day as they dismounted and went over to Brown, still beneath his machine. The hot engine had stalled and between them they managed to lift the machine upright and put it on its stand.

Stock retrieved his torch from his pocket and played the beam over Brown. From the odd angle of his head and the way it was twisted in his German helmet, it was obvious that his neck was broken. He crouched down and felt his neck for a pulse, but it was clear that he was dead. Had he been sitting at a desk, he would have held his head in his hands and moped over the catastrophe but instead he gritted his teeth, stood up and faced Day. "Don't say a word, Corporal. Anything you say won't help. And put that animal out of its misery." The deer was making disturbing snorting noises. "Quietly."

He turned his back on the scene and took a few paces out of the lights, needing time to think of the best way out of the awkward situation. He knew they should bury Brown and hide the bike, but sooner rather than later they would be found and reported. If to the Germans, they would likely raise an eyebrow as to what a British naval officer on a motorbike was doing so far inland. It wouldn't take them long to conclude that Brown was associated with the crystals and had been trying to retrieve them. From their noisy passage through the streets of Oisemont it would also be reported that there was more than one bike, and the hunt would begin. He checked his watch again and knew time was now even more significant, but he had two clear options: to bury Brown and hide his bike would take them the best part of an hour and would mean they would miss the first rendezvous with the MTB and therefore need to hide somewhere for the next twenty-four hours until it returned. And could they find somewhere to hide? On the other hand, if he left the scene just as it was, Brown might not be found until later in the day, or even the next, and that would give them enough time to find the briefcase, make the MTB and be gone before the manhunt began. The only problem was his uniform. A naval officer was definitely out of place, but if a Royal Engineer was found, then they might assume he was merely trying to reach the coast and not make the connection with the crystals.

Stock walked back to Brown's body, assessing that his own uniform might fit. Day was far too large.

"We're going to leave him here but swap his uniform with mine. There's no blood on it, only a tear on this leg. Quickly now, start undressing him and don't forget his dog tags," Stock ordered.

An uncooperative Brown was effectively now Lieutenant Stock as he put his own tags around the dead man's neck. They had not been updated to reflect his new rank. He also changed his wallet but removed the security pass first as he didn't want any reference to Godfrey being queried. He also kept his own new boots. It had taken far too long, but whoever found Brown would hopefully come to the conclusion that Stock hoped they would. There was a pervading smell of petrol from the leaking fuel tank and Stock briefly considered firing it to confuse the issue further but then thought the better of it for all sorts of obvious reasons. He finally did a quick search through the saddle bags and was surprised to find a silenced pistol in one of them and tucked it into his waistband. It was long and awkward which was presumably why Brown had left it there.

A bit out of breath, he reckoned they were about five miles from Oisemont, but he couldn't be sure, and he winced as he looked at his watch again, noting that they had little more than an hour and a half to reach the MTB. Righting his BSA he went to mount it and discovered the same problem that Brown had probably had, so he put the pistol in the saddle bag.

They resumed their path by turning right up a gentle incline and eventually, as the road levelled out, their beams highlighted their tree in the distance, but from the reverse angle that Stock was expecting. He felt a lot better now that he knew where they were. He cut across the grassy field and stopped next to the burn remnants of the barns and lorry. The undisturbed crater was there, and he could just make out the small mound where they had buried Rutherford. Stock knew exactly where to scrape his shovel and in less than two minutes was strapping the case onto his BSA. 'One hour left to do fifteen miles. Ought to manage that ok.'

He looked up as they started their bikes and saw that town of Oisemont had become more illuminated than before with more lights coming from all kinds of windows. Worse still, he saw some kind of vehicle emerging from the outskirts.

"Keep your light off," he barked at Day. He already had their route round Oisemont planned out in his head as it was the same as they had traversed a few days earlier. With Day in tow, as slowly and as quietly as the machine would allow, he moved off perpendicularly then away from the vehicle that was now accompanied by another. Worryingly, they were both heading in the direction of Brown. Glancing over his shoulder, he saw that they were a pair of German half-tracks and calculated that they would take at least five minutes to reach Brown, another five for assessment, plus five minutes to return to Oisemont and another five to phone ahead. A minimum of twenty minutes in all and that was assuming they could work out what was going on.

They were across the ditches. Once the last house was between them and the half-tracks, Stock turned on his light. Just in time too as there was a herd of deer less than a hundred feet directly ahead of them which scattered away in the blink of an eye. 'Bloody deer are more dangerous than the Jerries', but at least he recognised the route he wanted to take and, with Oisemont falling behind them over their left shoulders, he calmed down a little. The first time they had taken the same route, they had turned left soon after the main road, but this time they would go straight ahead. The main road was now Stock's main concern but there hadn't been a roadblock on their way through and he hoped there wouldn't be one now and he slowed them to a crawl as they approached it. To make sure their way ahead was clear he naturally looked left first but as he looked right, he saw a single headlamp in the far distance heading their way. 'Another motorbike; perhaps with a side car and machine gun mounted on it.' He had to assume it was German and without any delay, opened his throttle to cross the road before they would be in range of the oncoming bike's headlamp. He heard Day right behind him and in a few seconds reckoned they had two options: either keep their lights on and make a run to the coast, knowing that they could be followed by the sidecar until they ran out of dry land, or turn off their light and park up out of sight and wait for it to pass. He chose the latter. Thankfully, almost immediately on their right, was a stand of trees and bushes surrounding what turned out to be a small pond. Day copied his actions as he switched off his headlamp and stalled the engine before laying it down on the soft ground. Crouching, they watched the sidecar approach the crossroads and turn down the same road that they had just left, then pass them by but further down the main road and maybe three or four minutes away. They could see headlamps from several other vehicles approaching the crossroads. On the open and straight roads in the area, their taillights would have been easily visible, and Stock thanked his lucky stars that he had made the right decision.

"Here!" he whispered as he handed his revolver to Day. "Smash your rear light!" Stock did the same to his once Day had completed the simple task. "We'll give them a minute to get ahead but when we move off, you stay next to me on my left." Why he half-whispered he never knew. "If they are on the lookout for two bikes, and they see us approaching, they'll think it's a car."

While they listened to the sidecar's engine fade into the distance, Stock unfolded his map and hooded his torch on it, noting that if their way ahead was blocked they would have to divert through a small village which would be on their right in a few miles. Going sharp left was not an option as that would lead them away from Ault and over the Somme.

"We keep going straight down to Ault and ignore all other turnings. Ready? Let's get going then."

As fast as he dared with Day abreast of him, Stock led them past junctions, through the trees in the valley and up onto the small hill which was now shrouded in a clammy hill fog which dissipated as they lost height near the coast. There was one nasty moment when Stock had wanted to take the left-hand fork, even though it seemed the more minor road and he had to shout at Day as their machines nearly crashed into each other but now they were less than a mile outside Ault with just one more set of crossroads to go. Groaning inwardly, Stock saw the sidecar parked with its dull headlamp illuminating the junction. In the few seconds remaining before the Germans would realise their mistake, he made up his mind to risk it. Taking his right hand off the throttle, he unholstered his revolver, transferred it to his left hand and replaced his hand back on the throttle to catch up and slightly overtake Day. They were too close now for Stock to shout anything audible at Day without the Germans hearing an English voice, so he aimed his headlamp at the one soldier standing in the pool of light from the sidecar. The blinded soldier leapt out of the way, only to receive a glance from Day's machine but Stock had slowed and aimed his revolver at the German's headlamp and took two shots at it. The second hit.

He didn't know what the time was and guessed it was between four fifteen and four thirty and knew Ruddock would be on the lookout for them as he crossed in front of Ault. He hoped that, as long as they reached the tarmac road that ran parallel to the beach, that their headlamps would be visible from the sea, especially as they approached from their direction. He guessed they were being followed by the sidecar but, since it now had no headlights, they ought to have several minutes before it stood a chance of catching them up. As they turned right onto the coast road, he looked out to sea but couldn't see anything and instead concentrated on putting as much distance between them and the sidecar. Along way off to their right on what he presumed was another road, he saw a series of headlights heading towards Ault, now behind them.

If Ruddock wasn't there, then they were cornered. With relief, he saw the jetty just ahead and turned onto its wooden planking. He just had time to throw himself off the BSA before the front wheel skidded on the slippery timbers and he nearly followed it over the side onto the shingle a few feet below. Following as closely as possible, Day did exactly the same thing and Stock had to reach out his hand to stop him from falling onto both the machines which were now piled one on top of the other.

He reached into his pocket for his torch but found that it had been crushed which explained the sharp pain he now felt in his left hip.

"Your torch. Quickly!" he rasped at Day. Thankfully, this one worked, and he shone it at the two bikes. "Jump down there and fetch the case." He cloaked half of the beam so that it wouldn't shine sideways and saw Day shift the front wheel of his bike enough to unstrap the case from Stock's beneath it. Even while he watched this, he could hear the sidecar approaching but couldn't make out exactly where it was. Further inland, he could see a column of headlights still heading towards Ault. He held out his hand once again to help Day up onto the jetty. "Down the end but keep low." He doubted anyone would see them in the dark, but there was just the glimmer of dawn off to their right and he didn't want to take the risk. As they ran, or in his case limped, he pointed the torch out to sea, flickering the signal several times in different directions, and almost failed to see the end of the jetty; it was shorter than he remembered.

He pointed the torch down. Even though he had known the tide was going out, he was horrified to see just how far down the small waves were.

"Hand me the case and jump in. Let me know how deep it is." He was half-whispering again and didn't think to ask if Day could swim but there was no other choice left to them. Day sat down on the edge before letting himself drop the last foot and his head briefly disappeared. "About five feet. The case, sir."

Stock leaned over as far as he could, holding the lit torch in one hand so that Day could see it and let the case drop the short distance. "Make sure it stays dry." He let himself roll off the jetty making sure to miss Day as he submerged into the chilling blackness of the English Channel. "Hang onto these uprights for the moment. Here, take the case. Does that torch still work?" He couldn't remember if he had kept his hand up when he had dropped into the water and was extremely pleased with himself when he found that he had. Standing unsteadily and swaying in unison with the waves he wrapped his arm round one of the stanchions and flickered the signal out to sea again repetitively, straining his ears for the deep throb of the MTB's engines. Perhaps it was because he hadn't hooded the torch when he shone it down at the case or maybe because the sidecar crew had guessed his destination, but he could definitely hear it closer now. Nothing from seawards. He mused that it was ironic that they had both lost their BSAs over the side of the jetty and that they would be out of sight until at least dawn. But what then? If Ruddock didn't appear soon, they would have to make their way back inland and find shelter before much longer and he could already feel the cold taking a grip on him. From the note of the sidecar's engine, it seemed like it was passing the jetty by. He didn't look back as he knew it was still too dark to see, but there was a discernible lightening of the sky to the east.

With a sense of abandonment, he flicked the torch again: 'dot-dot-dash dot-dot-dot' and they waited while the cold sea tugged at their clothes.

"This case is getting bloody heavy," Day moaned. He was resting it on his shoulder. "But I'm ok for a while yet. What if…"

"Quiet!" Stock silenced him and repeated the signal. There it was again. Not the throb of the MTB, but out of the blackness the soft splash of an oar. The life raft appeared.

"Over here!" he whispered unnecessarily as it was almost on top of them. "Can you take the case first?"

"Can't see it," came the reply.

Stock hooded the torch again and made sure the rest of the beam shone away from the shoreline, but his fingers had started to go numb and as he fumbled, it slipped from his grasp into the water.

"It's ok, sir, they've got it." Stock then felt hands reaching for him, dragging him up into the small boat and, with the vague light behind him, saw that Day was scrambling into it as well.

"Right. Back to sea. Smartly now!" someone said in a firm but quiet voice and Stock felt the boat rhythm change with the direction of the waves.

"Mr. Roberts here, sir, coxswain with Commander Ruddock's compliments. Good timing if I may say so. We were just making our final run when we saw you come through the town. You did a fine job of disappearing those bikes quickly. There's a convoy of some sorts coming down the hill. Here, Rob, get those blankets out."

Stock nearly burst out in nervous laughter at the coxswain's comment about the BSAs but managed to check himself, trying to be professional. "Couldn't bring the boat in, what with the falling tide, and unless we hurry up, we've got a long row ahead of us as it's ebbing fast. Feeling warmer now, sir?"

Stock's teeth had started to chatter in the mild but cooling breeze on his sodden uniform and he could see that apart from Day and himself, there were three of them from the MTB. The coxswain steered while the other two put their backs into the oars. "Where's the case?" he asked anxiously.

"Between my feet, off the bottom," said Day opposite him.

"Still dry then?"

"Yessir. Made sure of it."

"Good job, Corporal. Well done."

"There's the boat," announced Roberts, adjusting the rudder to take the tide into account. Even the oarsmen looked over their shoulders to see just how far they would need to scull and preserve their energy. Stock then looked back at the now visible jetty and his heart sank when he saw that the convoy had stopped and was disgorging Germans right where their bikes were.

"I think we ought to get a move on, Coxswain," he said, motioning behind him. "We're still in range even in this light." They were only about a quarter of a mile offshore.

Roberts half turned to get a good look at the jetty and saw a machine gun on a tripod being unloaded from one of the trucks. "Pull, you buggers! We're not home yet," he urged. He reached into his duffle coat and pulled out a large torch which he pointed towards the MTB and tapped away in Morse. Dot. Dot. Dot. Dash. Dash. Dash. Dot. Dot. Dot. The international signal for SOS. Almost immediately they could hear the MTB's engines roar into life and Stock could imagine the scene aboard; the crew would already be at 'action stations.' Two of them would be manning the 20mm Oerlikon mounted near the bows and another the .303 Browning machine gun sited between the wheelhouse and the stern, both trained on the area where their signal originated. The chief engineer below decks would be making sure all the machinery continued to behave and the boatswain's mate would be at the wheel with Ruddock next to him with his binoculars trained on them. The last man, probably a leading seaman, would have the lead weight ready to fathom out their depth should it be necessary, and he was placed next to the Oerlikon crew, as being any further forward could mean he might be tossed overboard with the rising and falling of the powerful boat as it tried to cut a smooth passage through the waves.

The MTB had been almost stationary with its bows heading against the direction of the current until Ruddock had ordered 'steerage speed'. Under his guidance, it gracefully turned to port in a U-turn and headed towards them but slowed as it neared, allowing the leadsman to run to the bows and swing his lead forwards. Stock looked nervously towards the jetty and saw flashes from the end of it, and almost immediately the sea off to their right spumed in reaction to the bullets. Now that they were much further away, he had hoped that they would be out of range, and from the pattern of small splashes, it was clear that they nearly were, but the spuming water was getting much closer. A deeper more spaced series of bangs announced that the Oerlikon had opened fire on the jetty, its yellow tracer shells initially arcing high before lowering to zero in on the end of the jetty. Within a few seconds, the machine gun from shore had ceased firing. But now there was individual rifle fire and bullets plucked at the sea around them and one bullet clanged off one of the rowlocks, splintering the oar. The seaman fell onto his back as the strain on his 'pull' suddenly disappeared.

And then the MTB mercifully came between them and the shore, the sound of its Browning chattering loudly. A rope shot out from the deck towards them. Untangling himself from the blanket, Stock had the case in hand and passed it up to one of the outstretched arms while another was reaching for his other hand. He took the help and hauled himself over the edge and onto the flat deck.

"Out of the way, sir," a voice full of urgency shouted close to him. Initially on all fours, he scuttled away before standing up, then ducked as a bullet ricocheted off some nearby part of the boat. By the time he turned round to look down at their life raft, only the coxswain remained in it, and he was finishing off tying the rope before taking a hand up.

"Hold on," someone cried moments before the throttles of the MTB were fully opened and the boat surged forward. Stock was amazed at the acceleration and managed to grasp a railing on the side of the wheelhouse only just in time before he felt the salty spray cover him completely. It made him realise just how quick these MTBs were. Had he not been hanging on to something, he would by now be back in the sea, so for the moment he just clung on while the boat bucked against the waves. He didn't know it, but Ruddock was just above him in the wheelhouse and had been keeping his eye on him to make sure he didn't vanish over the side. A minute or so passed before the engine note reduced and the boat settled on a more even keel. He looked up in reaction to a voice.

"Glad to see you are still with us. Lieutenant?"

"Still here. Just."

"I think you can let go now. It's drier up here." There were no railings to hang onto along the side as he worked his way aft but there were some either side of the steep metal treads that led up to where Ruddock waited. Despite the MTB slowing down, the wind still cut through his sodden uniform, and he immediately started to feel its effects but was too proud to ask to go below straight away. It wasn't big enough to be called a Bridge, but he stood facing forwards, grasping the rail that ran the width with both hands while Ruddock ordered the throttles opened once again.

"You and your corporal are alright then, but I see you left Brown behind?"

"Had to. He's dead. Do you mind if I tell you out of the wind? It's damn freezing up here."

Although Ruddock was protected by his heavy coat, he appreciated how Stock was feeling and held out his arm, indicating that the soggier of the two of them should go first. Day was already in the cabin being helped into a duffle coat by one of the ratings and Stock gladly took the other that was offered to him. Ruddock had stayed behind to give the helmsman orders but now appeared and turned on the red night light, telling the rating to make himself scarce.

"We're well out of range now and I doubt they'll send out aircraft in this low cloud, but the lads are keeping an eye out. That was fine timing. Do you always keep your taxis waiting until the last minute?" Ruddock asked as he sat down on the bench opposite the pair of them without deploying the table, and to their joy, produced a hip flask which they gladly took in turn. He went on," White Star rum, slips down nicely don't you think?"

Stock wasn't sure if he was needling him or trying to alleviate the tension he and Day were experiencing, but decided it was the latter when the flask appeared. "Yes. A bit of a close-run thing. I think it was the noise of our BSAs on the way in that alerted them and those bloody deer nearly had us all. That's what killed Brown. Ran straight into him. Couldn't very well leave evidence of him being there, hence the swapped uniforms." He saw Ruddock's quizzical look. "Don't ask! Admiral Godfrey won't like it but thank you for being such a well-equipped taxi." He leaned forward, handed back the hip flask and then bent further to pick up the case that was on the floor. He put it on the bench between himself and Day. "I don't suppose it will matter you seeing this as it didn't mean much to me when I first saw it, but I've got to check it before we see the admiral. Corporal, I know you've earned the right, but I think it better if you look away for the moment."

He snapped the two catches, the back opening towards Day so that he couldn't see in without craning his neck and was relieved when he saw that it was still dry inside and very much as he remembered, although the papers were now very crumpled having been mashed between the rocks. He looked over and saw an impassive Ruddock looking into the case before he closed it. "Doesn't look much, does it? But apparently it's vital. I'm sorry Brown couldn't make it but at least his death hasn't been in vain. No doubt we'll all hear about its benefits sooner or later."

"I'm sure you'd tell me if you could and perhaps some other time?"

"Perhaps."

They both looked at each other, knowing it was unlikely they would meet again but for a brief moment, the spirit of comradeship bonded them together. They all grabbed whatever was at hand to stabilise themselves as the boat shuddered as it hit a larger wave and, before they could react, it hit another.

"Excuse me if I attend to other matters," Ruddock said as he looked up out of the doorway. "You two look like you could do with some sleep, and we've got a spare couple of hours so help yourselves. You'll rest easier on the tarpaulins in the ammunition locker through there." He pointed to the opposite end of the cabin.

Neither of them realised just how tired they were until they finished pulling the smelly tarpaulin about to make a rough mattress that would not only cushion them but help prevent them from rolling about. Stock placed the case under one of the folds to use as a bit of a stop for his body.

Day was lying on his back. He was so tired his voice was almost a murmur, "I had the feeling I wouldn't get on with Lieutenant Brown from the moment I met him. You know, you get these feelings if you like someone or not straight away and I just couldn't get comfortable with him. He kept me on edge, if you know what I mean. Not that I had much time to get to know him better, but he kept looking at me when we were loading, like he was deciding something. Made me feel like I wasn't wanted. Do you know what I mean, sir?"

Stock had his eyes closed, trying quite successfully to get some sleep but he found himself picturing their first encounter with Brown when he had entered the warehouse with the Admiral and wondered what might have passed between the two of them prior to their introduction. On the face of it, the admiral has supported Stock's request to bring Corporal Day along and Brown would have been already told about Day, but for what reason would there be enmity between Brown and Day? He hadn't felt anything, but then again, if Day had been the object of Brown's hostility, he wouldn't have anyway. Could it have been that the admiral didn't want someone as lowly as Day having even the faintest idea of what was going on and that Brown had been instructed to lose Day somehow in France? Was that why he had requested to take the rear of their procession so that he could somehow watch out for a chance to push Day into a ditch, or even kill him behind Stock's back? Perhaps if they were to be captured he was to ensure Day's silence, or it could have been that he just didn't like being 'piggy-in-the-middle.' Then another more sinister thought entered his mind. What if Brown had been ordered to kill both of them after they had dug up the case? His suspicious mind admitted that this was becoming a little far-fetched, but given the opportunity, he would raise the subject with the admiral when he explained how Lieutenant Brown had died. In the meantime, he needed to placate Day's fears and sleep on it.

"I know precisely what you mean, Corporal, but I think Lieutenant Brown was merely trying to be efficient. To him, we were strangers, and he was trying to assess our potential. You as a non-commissioned officer probably didn't gel with him, while I had authority that he couldn't challenge, even though he tried. Those types will always try to get one over on you, whoever you are. Goodnight and well done."

As he drifted off to sleep, he wondered whether, even if he did find out that Brown had had a sinister agenda, he could actually tell Day.

Chapter 9
Without Knowledge

Unattributably, as is common when surfacing from deep sleep, Stock wasn't sure if it was the change in the boat's movement or the coarse squawking from a seagull perched what felt like right next to his ear, but whatever it was, it was clear that they had berthed. The bump came again, and he knew then that it had been a combination that had stirred his subconscious from what felt like just five minutes' sleep. On the other hand, the oblivious Day was snoring loudly enough to accompany a brass band and he had to kick him twice before his larynx constricted enough to interrupt his cerebral thoughts.

A rating appeared holding two steaming cups of cocoa. "Mr. Ruddock's compliments, sir. The head's behind you."

"That was never two hours," exclaimed Day as Stock faded further into the gloom for his morning ablutions, but he gratefully took the two tin mugs and swore as one spilt onto his hand. "Shit!"

"Just what I had in mind, Corporal," Stock joked.

They shuffled round each other for a minute adjusting their uniforms that even when done would hardly have matched muster. Stock wished Brown's belt had an extra hole in it. When Ruddock saw them emerging he met them at the gangway. From the rings round his eyes, it was apparent that he had not enjoyed any sleep. "It was a pleasure to have had you on board, gentlemen." It was not the form of address he would have usually used for a mere corporal and, as Ruddock looked directly into his eyes, Stock realised that that one comment had made him feel that he really had earned his Stripes. Even more so when Ruddock held out his hand for Day to shake.

"Thank you, sir."

"I suppose you'll want to charge us next time?" Stock said with a smile.

"We only take tips, and then if it's just the infantry," Ruddock deadpanned back, looking over Stock's shoulder. "Looks like the admiral's sent a car for you. He's never done that for me." A black four-door Wolseley pulled up on the quayside a few yards from the gangplank and a young naval officer got out and held a door open. "Good luck with whatever you're doing with that case."

"You'll know about it soon enough," Stock smiled, shook his hand and saluted before leading Day back onto shore and towards the waiting car. Not a word passed between them and the driver, and within five minutes they were passing through the security gate at HMS Sultan.

The driver pulled up outside the same building where they had first met the admiral. "You know where to go don't you, sir? Second floor and you're to go straight in."

Passing through the open plan office that led through to Godfrey's, Stock noticed that there were now six people manning the desks, two of them on phones keeping their voices low, but there was no sign of the Wren. He knocked before they entered. Already seated off to one side was Mr. Morris who focused on the case Stock was carrying as he placed it on the floor next to his seat.

Godfrey directed them to the unoccupied chairs and let them sit in silence for a few uncomfortable moments while he decided what he was going to say. The third chair remained unoccupied.

"Will Lieutenant Brown be joining us?"

"No, sir."

"I see."

Stock thought he detected a hint of disapproval, but he couldn't be certain; he didn't know the admiral that well yet. The two hours' sleep was all that he had had, and he knew he would need all of his mental abilities in the presence of Godfrey.

"We'll come back to that later, but I see you have the case and from the look of it I take it that there's something worthwhile inside. Mr. Morris, if you please."

Mr. Morris stood up and took the heavy case from next to Stock and placed it on an empty space on the desk behind Godfrey. They all stared at its contents while Mr. Morris separated the crystals from the sheaf of papers, occasionally un-crumpling one or looking on the flip side of another. He stopped at one in particular.

"It's here. We've got it," he crowed and shook the piece of foolscap, waving it at Godfrey in confirmation. Then his eye was caught the next piece still in the case. "And here, here's the missing part we've been waiting for. This is tremendous, with this we can…" He had started hopping from foot to foot in excitement, but Godfrey stopped him.

"Thank you, Mr. Morris. Get your department working on it straight away. I'll take that, though," Godfrey said curtly and took the first piece of paper that Mr. Morris had been waving about and put it on his desk. "Corporal, would you go next door and ask Lieutenant Perris to come in, please."

"Lieutenant, accompany Mr. Morris back to the lab and make sure there's a guard on it and ask the others to make sure we're not disturbed for the time being. Corporal, will you wait outside while I have a word with Captain Stock here."

When the door finally closed and Godfrey had finished casting his eye over the piece of paper, he sat back and focused his eyes firmly on Stock. "Tell me what happened."

Stock kept it short, minimising a little the part about him getting them lost in Oisemont. He didn't try to disguise the timing to conceal the fact that Ruddock had stayed longer than he ought since he considered that Godfrey would find this out in any case. Godfrey had a clipboard in front of him and made an occasional note as the narration continued, and once he had finished asked him to go over his detailed reasoning behind the change of uniforms with Brown.

"Most thoughtful of you, most thoughtful. Certainly unorthodox, but not so obvious that it will be noticed anywhere and inadvertently you've done exactly the right thing, so the Germans definitely won't pick up on who he is…….or rather was."

"And who exactly was he?" Stock saw his chance to satisfy his curiosity and thought he saw Godfrey's eyes narrow a little at his question. "He was never going to be any use crossing the Channel, finding the way across France either there or back, or helping us to dig us the case. If there was going to be a fire fight our best chance of escape was always going to be stealth and speed, but having a third bike in tow was perhaps just one too many. I initially accepted your rationale of him joining us as our muscle man but if that is the case, in hindsight I must assume Lieutenant Brown's orders would have conflicted."

"You don't need to know what his orders were and if I decide a third man is needed, then a third man is needed. What would have happened if that deer had taken two of you off the road?"

Godfrey let him mull on that, but Stock knew then that there was more to it by the way he presented the 'fait accompli' argument and decided there was nothing to be lost by going on the offensive given that this was going to be his only chance to find out. "I accept without question your assessment, but would Lieutenant Brown have done the same?"

A frown of incomprehension crossed Godfrey's face. Whether or not it was for real, Stock would soon find out.

"Having previously returned with some of Rutherford's crystals proved that we were capable of doing the same again, in which case Brown's inclusion on our second visit was irrelevant. You must have known that, so what was Brown's real reason for accompanying us? After all, you hardly said a word to him in our presence in the warehouse, yet he knew precisely what he was supposed to do when we left."

"What I tell another officer in your absence is none of your business. Besides which, most of what is said around here is highly confidential and I'll remind you of that," Godfrey retorted. His voice now had an edge to it.

Stock felt a bit like a lawyer arguing a case. Ignoring these remarks, he continued, "On the boat on the way back, I asked myself if Lieutenant Brown would have sacrificed himself to enable me or Corporal Day to deliver the case to you. I think not. Being the arms expert that he was, how likely was he to be in need of a silenced automatic pistol? It wouldn't have been used in defence. You see, there's only one conclusion I can come to."

"You're overstepping the mark, Captain."

"I AM. Because I need to. I believe Lieutenant Brown had orders to kill Corporal Day and myself if there was a risk of us being captured. I can accept that, but it entered my mind that we were to be killed anyway just to protect the secret of those crystals. But now we're here and Brown isn't, and you've still got that dilemma. Yes, I suppose you could have me disappeared because I'm technically dead anyway, lying in a ditch somewhere in France, and you could have Corporal Day shot as a spy, but you have an entire crew of an MTB to consider as well as others in the Keppel's Head and that might take a bit too much effort on your part just to ensure your secret stays put. Against that you have to weigh up just how much of a risk is it with us still alive. Corporal Day knows virtually nothing, and I think I've more than established my loyalty, not to mention my usefulness. When we first met you described me as resourceful and promoted me to captain because of it. Or have I proved to be too resourceful?"

His tirade had not produced any reaction from Godfrey, and he hoped his effrontery wouldn't result in him and Day being immediately marched outside and shot.

Maintaining eye contact, Godfrey leaned forward and replaced his clipboard on the desk in front of him and replied in a very even tone. "Your vivid imagination is very much to your credit, and I don't suppose there's many others who could come to the same conclusion you've just done. On an almost daily basis, I have to make decisions with a prime objective in mind and judgements I make today might well mean someone a thousand miles away might die tomorrow. I have never had to justify my decisions to anyone other than myself and I'm certainly not going to change that now. One day I promote you from the lowliest rank of officers and the next you have the audacity to query my methods, so I put it to you, when you walk out of that door, will you be telling your corporal the outcome of this discussion?"

The background noises from outside the office didn't register with Stock as he wrestled with the complexities and intimations, and Godfrey allowed him time to reflect and arrive at the correct conclusion, at least from his own point of view. On the boat, he had already dismissed Day's concerns over Brown's behaviour, very much like the admiral was now dismissing his, and he didn't like it one little bit. He felt a little foolish and tried to maintain a straight face knowing that Godfrey would not know what he had already told Day. The question put to him hadn't entered his mind before and he realised he would never be able to tell Day, either one way or another.

"You see, there's more to command than just ordering someone to do something; that's the easy part. It's the reasoning behind that decision that's the real burden and it gets greater with rank, so if you don't like being a captain, I can always demote you back to second lieutenant.

Once again, Godfrey paused to let what he said to sink in. "I'm going to offer you some friendly advice, something I've not done to a junior officer before, but I think a person of your perception will be able to comprehend. Imagine yourself ten or twenty years from now sitting behind a desk such as this, and in front of you is someone you've just ordered behind enemy lines and you're fairly certain they'll never return. What encouragement would you be able to offer them? You certainly wouldn't give them the odds, would you? No, you'd more likely offer them some sort of aspiration to encourage the achievement of your aims but prepare yourself for the worst. In other words, have a contingency, always have a contingency. If I were you, Captain, I think I would let it rest there."

Stock recognised he was being given a final warning and it was apparent that Godfrey was never going to admit to his suspicions, but he effectively had his answer. Now that he had it, what was he going to do with it? Precisely nothing and Godfrey would have known that. Once again he felt humbled at being out-manoeuvred and realised he was never going to be able to hold his own against such a master. Time to follow advice and eat humble pie, look mollified and try not to break the thin ice he was on.

"Yes, sir, and thank you for your sound advice. Just one thing puzzles me though - were there enough crystals in that case to make enough sets?"

Godfrey considered Stock's question before picking up the piece of paper he had taken from Morris. "I'm told there's enough for the time being but here's the name of the boat that's due to dock at Liverpool with a significant quantity of the ore on board described as 'rock samples', as long as it isn't sunk before it gets there. To save you wondering further, Rutherford and some other fellow found this quartz in a mine in Mexico before the war, but due to the country's neutrality and German interference, couldn't obtain an export licence, so they arranged for some to be smuggled out; that's what's on the boat. What you brought back was just what Rutherford had managed to put in his luggage. It somehow ended up in Paris. Of course, all this is pretty irrelevant if Mr. Morris can't get it to work properly and there's no harm in letting you know that part of it. After all, you know the rest."

"Mr. Morris seemed over the moon just now. Do you think he'll take long to have it up and running?"

"I hope not. We're losing too many ships to those bloody U-boats." He shuffled papers into a buff file on his desk and opened another that he retrieved from behind him. "Now, another problem. What to do with you."

"In what way, sir?"

"You're supposed to be dead, remember? Technically speaking, you died this morning from a motorbike accident in France. If it isn't recorded, the Germans might pick that up. You did say you swapped the dog tags, didn't you?"

"Yes, and the wallet but I've got your security pass here." He reached into his back pocket and produced the slip.

"Well done. Hang onto that for the moment. I think we have two options here. One is to leave you dead and for you to assume Lieutenant Brown's persona. The other is to just ignore it and presume that the Germans overlook it which they probably will, due to your lowly rank. Any first thoughts?"

He didn't really like the idea of impersonating someone else, and even less, abandoning his family name, but he could see Godfrey's point that it was a loose end that might have repercussions at a later date.

"There's a third option. When I changed dog tags with Lieutenant Brown, mine still reflected my rank as second lieutenant even though the uniform was a captain's. The quartermaster hadn't had time to make my new tags, and if you think about it, that's probably not that uncommon anyway, must happen quite often in the field. You could believably record Second Lieutenant Stock's death while I still maintain my own identity. It wouldn't even need a change of service number as I gather they're doubled up between regiments."

For the first time, Stock saw a slight smile on Godfrey's face. "You're quick, aren't you? I'm glad I asked. Yes, that's the simplest solution." He scribbled on a note pad. "We can't announce it too soon, but we'll get something in next week's Telegraph. If you're writing home, better tell them you've noticed it and that it's not you. That'll stop any queries. Well done again."

By now, Stock was beginning to feel he'd had enough of the intensity of the admiral's office and was hoping to be dismissed, but where to? He still didn't know where his unit was and was about to ask when Godfrey held up his index finger as he looked down at the open file on his desk.

"I suspect you'll be wanting to return to your unit, and you'll be pleased to know most of them have made it back and are reforming near East Grinstead in West Sussex at Hobbs Barracks." He looked up to see Stock's reaction. "But I have another job for you before I let you go. Tonight, if you feel up to another excursion?"

This time he couldn't but help show his emotions and for a few moments his jaw dropped but he slowly closed it. Apart from wanting a bit more sleep and a few bruises here and there, he felt fine, and he tried to think what special talents he had that Godfrey could possibly want, and once again at short notice. The air between them had obviously cleared and he must still hold his trust, but he was intrigued and began to wonder if it there was an ulterior motive. "Will it involve the likes of Lieutenant Brown and has it got anything to do with crystals?"

"Not this time and no, there is nothing nefarious, but in a roundabout way, you have chosen yourself for what I'm about to ask you to do."

He was completely baffled and the puzzled look on his face must have said it all.

"When the British expeditionary force was dispatched to France last year, its main supply port was Calais, but it soon became apparent that it would need a secondary port, a backup if you like, and Dieppe was chosen. Shortly before the evacuation was ordered we were still sending over supplies mainly through Dunkirk and Calais, but it was felt that these two were a little too close to the front lines so more and more equipment was being sent to Dieppe. That included fuel. In fact, most of the fuel went through Dieppe anyway as that's where the main storage tanks are. It's very convenient as the fuel is refined at Fawley, just down the road from here, and it takes very little time for a tanker to cross the Channel. In anticipation of pushing the Germans back and having extended supply lines, less than a month ago we sent three tankers over there and filled up the storage tanks to capacity with petroleum spirit, and that's on top of the thousands of forty-gallon drums also stored there. Annoyingly, we could do with that fuel here right now, but we don't have the wherewithal to retrieve it and, seeing that the evacuation will be over shortly, the last thing we want to do is make Jerry a gift of half a million gallons of fuel."

Stock was stunned at the apparent lack of coherent planning as he had been brought up believing that the British army was the best in the world and that the likes of the generals and field marshals were people who knew exactly what they were doing. From what Godfrey had just said, someone somewhere had been negligent and was leaving it up to someone else to sort out. He tried to imagine what half a million gallons looked like but gave up.

"As you and your corporal are the closest people with any kind of knowledge about blowing up fuel dumps, I'd like you to return to Dieppe and fire it - or as much of it as you can."

Godfrey could almost see the workings of Stock's mind as he tried to work out the whys and hows but decided to save him the time. "You see, we can't send in the navy to shell it as the Prime Minister has forbidden anything larger than a frigate anywhere near the French coast and those that are being used are tied up with getting as many personnel away from Dunkirk as possible before the Germans overrun it. We can't ask the Royal Air Force because of the weather right now. Anyway, most of it has been destroyed. What's left is being used as cover for our ships, and besides which what's needed is a bomber but if we did send up a squadron they wouldn't stand a chance against the Luftwaffe's new fighters. We can't ask our chaps in Dieppe to destroy it as I learned last night that they've had to surrender, probably to the same bunch you came across, and on top of that the experts in the Royal Ordnance Corps who were sent over to do the job, according to you, were blown up with the ship you saw in Dieppe harbour."

Despite it being only a few days ago that he and Day had made their escape, he couldn't remember seeing anyone from the ROC on the quayside and mentally kicked himself for not being more observant, but he did vaguely recall seeing unusual items being unloaded just before it exploded. In mitigation, he admitted he did have other more pressing items on his mind at the time, like staying alive.

Godfrey continued, "I can't get a replacement from our ordnance headquarters in Bicester in time who has a clue about demolition and the rest of them are scattered throughout the south-east of England on their way back from France. We need someone with experience and not just in blowing up fuel. We need someone's who's familiar with Dieppe. Can you recall the layout there at all?"

Stock was managing to keep up as Godfrey revealed more of the sorry story and realised it was incumbent upon him to accede to Godfrey's request for him to go back to Dieppe. He shut his eyes and tried to visualise the devastating scene he had left behind. The only time he had had to look around was when they were in the ferry. He recalled the broken bridge over to the island, the rocky outcrop, the upturned boats and… and… yes, on the far bank not far from the burning warehouses something that looked like a depot, but were those stacked drums? Maybe. And was that a pumping station further along?

"I think I know where it might be, but perhaps Lieutenant-Commander Ruddock may also be able to help. I presume he's been in and out of Dieppe a few times?"

"You're quite right and that's how we're going to get you to and from France again. You'll be quite at home in that MTB, won't you?" A half-chuckle from Godfrey lightened the otherwise serious atmosphere.

"I've been asked by the Ministry of Supply to make sure that that fuel doesn't fall into enemy hands and I'm sorry to ask you so soon, but we have to get this done tonight before they have a chance to secure the compound. Also, the tide timing is against us but you're well aware of that, aren't you? The commander of the small garrison we had at Dieppe was killed in one of the air raids and his second-in-command was in contact with us when the Germans suddenly cut him off. From what he was saying at the time, it looks like just an advance formation, but if we leave it by more than just a few hours, then we may never be able to get anywhere near that fuel. I am sure you realise that."

'Here we go again' thought Stock, nothing like being in the right place at the right time. "I don't suppose there's a floorplan of that depot, is there?"

"Unfortunately, not. The only person with that knowledge was in that ship when it went up, so you'll just have to make do, but we do have a chap coming up from Fawley to describe the layout in our refinery and that might give you a clue as to what to expect."

"And what about explosives? I really don't want to rely upon shooting bullets again."

"We're working on that at the moment, but it looks like you'll be using an amatol-based substance. It's more waterproof, in case you get wet on the way in. Just lately, the Ordnance Corps have been experimenting with stronger magnets for their limpet mines, you know, underwater mines you put on the hull of a ship, but you won't be using those as we haven't got any yet, and anyway, they're a bit too heavy; but it'll be something similar and probably magnetic. I'm calling a briefing at 18.00 this evening, Room P again, so go and get some rest at the Keppel's Head and save any more questions for then. Lieutenant Perris will take you there. Ask him to come in on your way out, will you?"

He rose from his chair but hesitated on his way to the door. "Just one thing for the moment, sir. I'm sorry about Lieutenant Brown but I'll stay in his uniform for the time being if that's alright with you."

Godfrey was already looking into the contents of another file and Stock had the impression that if he'd had a coffee cup in hand right then, he would have spilt it. "Of course. Silly of me to overlook such an obvious thing. Go ahead."

The speed at which Godfrey had terminated their meeting caught Stock by surprise and he supposed that there were other urgent matters that needed his attention, but at least he had come away still a captain, even if it might be for just another day. He was reluctant to reveal to Day some of what the admiral had said to him while still in the confines of the spartan waiting room. Anyway, Lieutenant Commander Ruddock was there, and had clearly been waiting for some time from the way he looked at him on the way through. It wasn't until they were back in his room at the Keppel's Head that he told Day what to expect over the forthcoming night, and - exactly as Godfrey had predicted - he didn't mention anything about Lieutenant Brown.

Chapter 10

Timing – Part I

He almost overslept because the bloody landlord hadn't woken him, and it was only due to his unconscious sixth sense did he wake up just in time and rush to the room opposite to shake some life into a snoring Corporal Day. They had both enjoyed deep sleep after a relatively sumptuous lunch which had included too many potatoes, but at least they had been hot. For no particular reason he had wanted them to be seated in Room P when the others, probably including Ruddock again, arrived. It turned out that he was beaten to it, and he had barely finished adjusting his chair when the admiral walked in, accompanied only by the Wren. No Lieutenant Browns this time, but in his place, a smart-looking civilian sat biting his nails like a nervous child.

"Good evening, gentlemen. Almost the same as yesterday, isn't it? You won't have met Mr. Longton before; he's from the Esso oil refinery at Fawley and will tell you what layout to expect when you get there." He turned to his Wren to ask, "Has he signed the official secrets act yet?"

"I have it here, sir," she replied, producing a folder and a pen which she opened and placed in front of Longton, who immediately signed it. Stock wondered what would have happened if he hadn't. Before she sat down, she unrolled and weighted down the same chart of the Channel they had used yesterday and Stock saw outlines of the erased chinograph lines that had depicted their course.

"Tonight's objective is to destroy the fuel depot at Dieppe. Messrs. Stock and Day here will need to know the best places to lay the charges, which is why Mr. Longton is with us." Stock noted that the admiral purposefully hadn't referred to his rank.

Longton ceased gnawing at his thumbnail at the mention of his name and produced a single piece of folded paper. "Oh, yes, I've drawn a sketch of what to look out for. Look here!" He placed it in the centre of the table at pointed at it. "Fawley is the biggest refinery in Europe and we at Esso are very proud to have all the latest technology, including the newest pumps that measure in tonnes rather than gallons. Like any refinery, it needs a feed from the seaward side for the tankers to connect to and it's not just a simple case of pumping the oil. It has to go through a filtration plant first before it reaches the primary storage area, and from there pipes will take it to the atmospheric mixing tank before being split into various elements and…"

"I think we need to know the best place for placing the charges rather than a lecture in refining, so can you get to the point and remember this is not a refinery, just a depot," snapped Godfrey.

"Oh, ok. Er, well, you see there are always shut off valves between each element, just in case there's a fire, and you really ought to open those first so that the fire can spread quickly. Basically, if you choose the biggest tank on the highest ground and open the purge valve, then whatever's in it will flow downhill and affect the rest. That doesn't guarantee it will all go up as normally it's on level ground, so I'd say the isolating valves are the things to go for. Oh, and if you can blow the main input valve where the ships discharge, that'll be a bonus as you might get a back-surge and destroy the ship as well." Longton looked up and beamed, but his oration did not have a reciprocal effect and he quickly wiped the smile off his face.

"Thank you Mr. Longton. Any comments?" Godfrey was looking to Stock as he was going to be the man in place, and he had never been to a refinery or a fuel depot of this size. He was trying to picture what he might come up against so he could ask the right questions.

"How big are these valves and how easy are they to turn?"

"Oh, I'd say about this big." Longton held his arms out like a fisherman boasting about his latest catch. "And the valves ought to be of the standard gate valve type with big wheels on top. You may need a monkey wrench to get them to turn if they haven't been maintained properly. Er, come to think of it, you'll need a big wrench in any case. Sometimes it takes two men to shift some of our valves, and we have a special crowbar for doing just this. Oh, and look out for the security locks on them. Some of them have tabs that stop you from turning them without releasing them first. In which case, you have to turn a lever at the base of the valve so that it will release the wheel."

"Can we have two of your bars to take with us?" Stock asked.

"Oh, er, well, I suppose so," Longton stuttered.

Godfrey interrupted. "I'll send someone down with you. Arrange that, will you?" He motioned with his hand to the Wren. "Now, unless there's anything else I think you ought to get straight onto that as time is rather short. Thank you, Mr. Longton."

The Wren was already on her feet and pulling back Longton's chair, but he paused before he had taken a step. "Oh, there's just one other thing. You really don't want to be anywhere nearby when it goes. I mean there'll be a heck of a bang when it does go up."

Virtually in unison Stock and Day let out truncated laughing noises.

"Goodbye, Mr. Longton," the admiral urged as the Wren was already ushering the man out through the door.

Stock felt he had to add to Longton's last statement. "He's certainly right about that. It's difficult to explain the power of exploding petrol, more so to imagine it and unless you've actually experienced it, you can't imagine how quickly everything happens, and how what you don't expect also happens. The corporal and I learned that very quickly last week."

Godfrey retrieved a cigar shaped metal case from his pocket and handed it to Stock. "I'm glad you brought that up because this is a dummy casing of what you'll be using. The detonator." He let him play with it for a few moments and let him hand it to Day before continuing, "That'll be filled with amatol and fixed to a block of dynamite. If you screw the top, you'll feel it clicking. Each click represents two minutes; twist it all the way and it'll give you a maximum of thirty minutes. Try it if you like." Day did so gingerly and held it up. Godrey went on, "It's chemical not clockwork so you won't hear anything, but you see there's a slit in the side which'll be mated to the dynamite. You can tie the whole thing to the valves with the cord that comes with it. There'll be a dozen of them waiting for you at the armourer's."

"I think as far as you are concerned, Mr. Ruddock, you will almost be able to repeat yesterday's visit but with a little adjustment in place and timing, don't you think?

"I've already looked at the charts and I don't think there'll be any problem seeing that there's no sand bar this time, but as Dieppe is a little further west and we're twenty-four hours later, high tide'll be nearer 01.00. What dropping off point did you have in mind, sir?"

"I was hoping you could tell us that. It's no use even contemplating sailing into the harbour so you're going to have to pick a point somewhere off to the west. Stock seems to remember the depot is on that side of the estuary and they won't want to go through the town to get to it."

"We refuelled once from the island mid-channel, but I can't recall where the main depot was. There are some cliffs along this part that finish about here and that's less than a mile from the quay, otherwise it's sandy beach all the way. How about just under these cliffs a bit further along? They're higher there and our rubber life raft ought to be able to slip in there quite nicely," Ruddock suggested.

"I agree. Now, timing: let's assume it's going to take you an hour from the landing point to the depot, half an hour to get in, half an hour to lay the charges and another hour to return. That's three hours in all but add on half an hour just in case. Do you think you two can manage that?" From the look on Godfrey's face, he was almost daring Stock or Day to disagree.

"Sounds about right to me, sir, but it will depend upon us locating the right places for the charges."

Godfrey thought about this for a moment before responding, "Fair enough. Let's say four hours in all then, two hours either side of high tide. You'll want to land at 23.00 which means you'll be leaving here by 20.00. I take it your boat is still fully operational?"

"Apart from needing another life raft, yes. It's already been refuelled and rearmed."

The door opened and closed again as the Wren returned. "Lieutenant Martin is accompanying Mr. Longton and will be taking the wrenches directly to the boat, sir," she addressed Godfrey.

"Thank you, Lieutenant. In a minute I'll ask you to take these two to the armourer." He indicated to Day that he wanted the cigar case back. "I'm going to issue you with silenced pistols as they'll be the most effective weapon if you come across any guards. You'll also have wire cutters, torches, and a few other handy items. Any more questions?"

To Stock, it all sounded so simple as they sat round the large table, but he knew it would be a problem finding the depot in the dark and more difficult finding the right valves in the depot, but there would be little to be gained by airing his concerns.

Godfrey stood up. "Good luck, gentlemen, and I'll see you two in my office when you return." He looked at Stock before turning to the door at the rear of the building. "This time I'll be needing a written report."

Outside there were two cars with drivers waiting for them.

"I'm glad you're not the seasick type. It's going to be a bit rougher out there tonight so no cocoa this time," Ruddock grinned.

"Never liked cocoa much anyway. By the way, did you really need another life raft? I thought you brought the other one back?"

"You wouldn't have seen it, but we lost it when we took off from Ault. Close call last night as it was probably a bullet that cut the line. Anyway, it was about time we had a new one as the old one was looking a bit patchy."

Stock saw the Wren itching to get away but couldn't resist quipping, "Not to mention your rowlocks being shot away."

"Now, now, no need to get offensive. We all have our shortcomings. See you down there," Ruddock chuckled at the innuendo but as he got in his car a verse from a song started rattling round his head. He decided he enjoyed Stock's company.

I don't want to join the army, I don't want to go to war
I'd rather hang around Piccadilly underground,
living off the earnings of a high-born Lady
I don't want a bullet up the arsehole,
I don't want my rowlocks shot away
I'd rather stay in England, merry, merry England
And fornicate my bloody life away.

Chapter 11
Timing – Part II

When they arrived at the MTB's berth, he and Day had viewed the two crowbars placed besides the gangplank. They were massive, made of solid iron about six feet long with a pair of lugs protruding nearer one end. Stock went to pick one up with one hand but needed two.

"How the hell are we expected to lug these bloody shafts about as well as our packs? Must weigh thirty pounds or so," he asked Day rhetorically.

The packs provided by the armourer were already filled with six of the charges in each as well as various other tools, including a length of rope a-piece. Obviously, someone had been given the impression that they were to be attempting a rock face. In addition, they had been handed a pair of four-foot bolt-croppers. He did a quick calculation: each pack weighed around sixty pounds, croppers another ten. With the bars it totalled nearly a hundredweight, and this was on top of the grenades attached to their webbed belts. The silenced pistols were in purpose-made long leather holsters that nestled partly beneath their left arms.

So, before they moved off from the quay while the boat wasn't rocking about too much, they rationalised their packs in the shelter of the cabin. They discarded one of the lengths of rope, all the hammers and cleats, and other such climbing equipment that Stock decided was not going to be needed. When they finished, they had much more manageable packs.

The bracing south westerly wind buffeted anything it could as the MTB motored down Southampton water at a steady pace. Ruddock pointed out that they would be passing Fawley refinery on the starboard side and diverted closer so Stock and Day could take a good look from the bridge. At Stock's request he ordered the throttles back to a crawling pace as he was having difficulty focussing on the big pipes that lay on top of the long jetty. He was awed at the size of the entire facility behind. The first thing he noticed were the tall towers that backdropped the round storage tanks, interconnecting with differing sizes of tubes and pipes and resembling an ill-made spiders web. He concentrated on those that fed the jetty. He lowered the binoculars as Ruddock closed on it. Looking up at the termination points no more than fifty feet away, he hoped that the explosives they had been given were going to be powerful enough to punch holes in the metalwork.

"It's been pretty much abandoned since last September," offered Ruddock. "Too close to France and too easy a target for the Luftwaffe but some is still stored here. Just back there is where we refuel."

"How thick are those pipes?"

"Oh, I'd say less than quarter-plate size, eighth of an inch, maybe more, but remember they traverse quite a distance and the middle point between the flanges is where they are weakest. You need to go for those valves - see them?" he asked, pointing towards the base of the jetty where six pipes joined manifolds on top of which were six corresponding spoked wheels. There were more behind them. In fact, everywhere Stock looked there seemed to be big shut-off valves.

Stock raised the binoculars and lowered them again. "Yes, there's plenty of them, aren't there? It's all very well being able to see in which direction the pipes go in daylight but even now I couldn't tell you which one does what. And it's going to be black as hell tonight, not the mention that we won't be able to use our torches otherwise they'll soon be onto us."

Ruddock sympathised with his dilemma. "Look at those pairs over there. You can see the safety levers Longton was talking about, but they're not on the others over there. If I were you, I'd try them first."

Through the binoculars, Stock could see a lever that protruded through the spokes of a wheel, preventing it from being turned. Unless a counter motion was applied to the wheel first, the lever could not be moved out of the way, but once it was clear, there would be nothing to stop the wheel unwinding the valve it was attached to.

Ruddock ordered a change of direction and speed towards France. "Most people would give their right arm to be given the opportunity to blow up a fuel depot, but I certainly don't envy your task tonight, but look on the bright side," he paused, waiting for Stock to appreciate what he was thinking, but it was Day who guessed first.

"We'll be a lot lighter on the way back!"

Stock groaned at the obvious and grabbed at a rail as the MTB bucked as it gathered speed. "Let's get below before we get soaked."

Once they were seated, Ruddock deployed the table and produced a detailed chart of Dieppe with lines already drawn.

"We'll approach the cliffs further from the west on 105 degrees this time and drift in on the current. Ault's about another ten miles further along off this chart. I can't land you directly on the beach below the cliffs, but I ought to be able to get within a thousand feet or so, maybe less, and the dingy will take you the rest of the way. Because of the choppy sea, we can't zip across the Channel as fast as we'd like, but we're slightly ahead of schedule so still aim to disembark you at 22.00, and the same as yesterday goes. We'll stand off a few miles until about 02.00 and drift in again, so when you signal, point your torch along this sort of line. Ok?"

"Same as before. US?"

"May as well."

Ruddock looked at the pile of discarded equipment in the corner and called for a rating to move it into one of the lockers. He continued, "From memory, the cliffs are about a hundred feet high, but if you go slightly to the east towards Dieppe, I think you'll find they peter out and I seem to remember there being tracks cut into them. With any luck you won't need your ropes and climbing kit."

"That's what we're relying on as well. I've taken some of the climbing equipment out of our packs or they'll slow us down. When we escaped on the ferry, those cliffs were quite a long way away from the harbour but then everything looks further away in the mist. The admiral forgot to ask me if I could climb."

"The admiral kept you for quite a time, didn't he?" Ruddock looked more closely at Stock hoping for an explanation as to why he was still dressed in a naval lieutenant's uniform.

Stock understood the veiled question and fingered his lapel. "Just wanted to know more about Lieutenant Brown's death. Anyway, I expect the quartermaster would have raised more than just an eyebrow if I'd walked in there again and asked for another uniform two days in a row. Probably wouldn't have had my size again in any case."

"If it's not too awkward, what were you doing in Dieppe in the first place?"

Stock told him about his posting to an airfield and their exploits when left behind to destroy the remaining fuel, but he left out any reference to Rutherford even though Ruddock already knew there had been someone else involved. "That's why the admiral wanted us to attend to this depot. It's called being in the wrong place at the wrong time. The same goes for you, doesn't it?"

"We were quite enjoying Jersey, escorting minesweepers up and down the Channel and intercepting the occasional E-boat. We once had a go at a U-boat and actually hit him with the Oerlikon a few times before he submerged but we lost him. I don't suppose what you were doing had anything to do with the new ASDIC sets, did it?"

"We're not supposed to talk about it, but yes. I imagine you'll soon find out anyway. With any luck, you'll have the chance to track those U-boats underwater, but you haven't got any depth charges on board, have you?"

"Not yet, but the shipyard manager I was talking to a few days ago was preparing sets of ramps. Never did find out what they were going to be used for, but they looked about the same size that would take a depth charge barrel. Then we got called away to help with the evacuation."

A cry for above brought Ruddock to his feet and he disappeared through the cabin door. He returned a few minutes later. "Looks like Jerry's getting bolder. One of the lookouts spotted a pair of E-boats heading towards Cherbourg but they didn't see us with the darkness behind us. There's not much chance of you getting any rest this time in this rough sea, but I'll leave you to it."

He returned to his bridge.

Both Stock and Day were beginning to feel the effects of being cooped up in the cabin as the MTB bucked it way through a heavy sea. Stock in particular was wondering if he was going to embarrass himself by being sick and looked just once towards where the head was. Ruddock had ordered all lights out but for a single small red one by the navigating desk as this didn't impair their night vision when returning to the open deck. Eventually, the note of the engines fell to a burble as the boat slowed but did nothing much to help the sickening movement so Stock decided they would be better off on deck.

Ruddock concentrated on peering through his binoculars straight ahead and they waited until he lowered them. "Jerry must think he's immune from attack. You can see they've left some lights on in Dieppe. Here, look for yourself."

His night vision was not yet as attuned as those who were already on deck, but Stock was handed a second pair of binoculars by someone. Once he managed to stabilise them in rhythm with the boat, he saw what Ruddock meant.

"How far away are we?"

"About fifteen thousand feet or three miles to you. This current ought to take us to those cliffs off to the right. See them?"

Stock adjusted the focus a little and could see the luminesce of the perpendicular chalk cliffs that extended past them. "We're aiming for where they finish, right?

"Just before. With this following wind our sound will carry in that direction, so we've got to watch it. Even our voices may be heard so keep it quiet. When we pick you up, I've told the lads to strike directly offshore. Our drift will hopefully meet you just beyond your drop off point." He leaned over the side and said something to those below. "Won't be long now. They're loosening the stays on the raft so get your kit up onto the aft deck. Oh, and by the way, I recommend you remove your socks and boots until you reach the shore, otherwise you'll be sliding around all over the place."

They struggled the heavy packs up through the cabin doorway. Stock was glad they had left the iron bars up there. It was only when they were waiting for the final order to release the raft's stays that he noticed that all signs of seasickness had gone. At a word from Ruddock, the raft slid over the side. Two ratings adeptly dropped into it and held out their hands to receive their packs before they got in. Stock heard a distinctive splash as he was positioning himself towards the front; one of their bars had been fumbled in the dark and was now resting on the bottom of the sea. There was no cursing or exclamations, only whispers. Moments later, someone handed him the second bar which he carefully placed on the bottom of the raft. In retrospect he ought to have got the crew to feel the weight of those bars as they were uncommonly heavy to the unsuspecting, especially in the dark.

The wind was strong enough to whip a little spray into their eyes and it became more pronounced as they approached the overhang of the cliffs. As the two oarsmen sculled, he looked at the narrowing gap between them and the white cliffs that radiated brighter the closer they got. Before he knew it, they were bottoming out, still several feet from the shore. They all got out and pulled at the raft's ropes to beach it. Next to him, he felt more than saw Day go down on his front and briefly semi-submerge in the breaking waves.

"Good luck," whispered one of the ratings and then they were gone, leaving them alone on the shore.

Stock and Day helped each other on with their packs. Day volunteered to take the iron bar which he crossed over his shoulders, draping his hands towards each end. Although their night vision was now well established in the cloudy, virtually moonless night, they could only just make out the undulations in the tussocks that lay ahead. Stock carefully guided them inland up a steep chalky path, keeping the shore over his left shoulder. Keeping their balance was the biggest challenge.

Day was experiencing far more difficulty as his sodden uniform was twice the weight. His breath rasped so much so that, after only two minutes, Stock had to relieve him of the iron bar. Sea water had partially penetrated their boots somehow, so they had to check each step they took was secure before transferring weight to the other leg. Consequentially, their initial pace was woefully slow and twice more they stopped to rest before reaching the top. Had there been a sentry anywhere nearby, even though he wouldn't have been able to see them, he would have assumed he was being invaded by a bunch of asthmatics.

Eventually, they sat down and relieved themselves of their packs. Once they got their breath back, they looked over to make out the port of Dieppe lying beneath them. As Ruddock had pointed out, the Germans had not yet imposed a Blackout. Lights twinkled here and there and part of the quayside was well and truly illuminated. They could see a low stone wall less than a hundred yards in front of them, which presumably marked the outskirts of the town. Mercifully, it was all downhill.

Stock felt for the binoculars in his pack and steadied them on it, looking for the tell-tale stubby round towers of the depot. It took him a couple of minutes to see the outline of one protruding from behind a three-storey building.

He handed the binoculars to Day and whispered, "I think that's it just to the left of the square shaped building." It was no use pointing in the dark and he waited for Day to confirm he'd seen it.

"Got it."

"Ready?"

Day returned the binoculars. He was just reaching for his pack when he froze; footsteps were coming their way. He gripped Stock's arm firmly and squeezed. Less than two minutes ago, they had been trying to breathe as much as humanly possible, but now the reverse was true as they both peered into the gloom to try and make out exactly from which direction they had heard the steps. They had both heard the footfall thuds but now they were gone. Then there they were again but a bit nearer. They still couldn't make out anyone out.

Very slowly, Stock rolled over and unclipped the top of his holster and palmed the pistol, pointing it in the general direction. He readied his torch in the other hand, and waited, waited, straining his ears, but nothing came.

"What do you think, Corporal?"

"Someone's out there but I just can't see him."

He waited a little more. "We can't just lie here. Leave the packs. On my mark, you go right, I'll go left. Got your pistol ready?"

"Oh, yes."

"Then don't forget the safety catch." He was about to say Go! when they heard multiple thuds and the tinkering of a bell. Stock felt like a jackass as he rose and flicked on the torch to reveal a goat balefully looking directly at them from only a few feet away.

"Bloody hell, just a damn goat."

"Nearly ended up as goat stew," Day added, putting his pistol away.

"Enough of this, come on. Let's get these packs on. You first." They struggled into them, Day muttering just audibly, "Nearly gave me a bloody heart attack. Ruddy goats! I suppose his mates will be along soon and if they're not careful I'll bloody have them, skin them alive, crush their…"

"Sssshhhhh. Remember there might really be a sentry about."

Gingerly, they made their way towards where the wall ended, passing between two houses that led to a narrow broken-cobbled street. Nothing stirred and nobody was about, not even a barking dog. Stock kept them at a slow pace, staying in the middle of the path. His mind briefly wandered back to the previous few days when they had been doing exactly what they were doing now, only then it was on motorcycles and a mistake could quickly be rectified. Now, if they took a wrong turn it would take them a lot longer. Not that they could see much in the dark, but they could no longer see the depot hidden behind buildings.

Stock tried to keep their bearings as the street widened and meandered, all the while trying to memorise their route for the way back. Faced with the inevitable T junction, he could only guess; both went downhill and veered away. He chose the one off to the right for no particular reason. He reasoned that as long as they continued downhill, they would eventually come out somewhere along the quayside and be able to locate the depot from there. As luck would have it, they unexpectedly came across it; it was directly across the road right in front of them on the other side of a high stone wall.

All of a sudden, the moon made a bright but brief appearance, long enough for them to see that the wall continued for some way off to the left. There was an alleyway running down the side of it off to the right. They scuttled into the shadows of a house. Then, with hardly a pause, they headed for alleyway.

The ground had nearly levelled off and the stink of rotting fish grew stronger with every step as they made their way down the alley strewn with rubbish. Then they could smell the distinctiveness of fuel; diesel at first, then the faint whiff of petrol. As the wall continued, they realised they were not going to find a way in along this flank. Ahead it terminated at a road which turned out to be peripheral to the quay. Stock carefully looked round the corner. Fortunately, it was only the other side of the estuary that was lit; where they wanted to go was well in the shadows, far away from the occasional figure that Stock supposed was the patrolling guard detail. He looked to his left, trying to see if there was one guarding the entrance to the depot. After only a few feet, the stone wall finished and in its place was a sturdy metal railing fence that ran parallel to the west quay. They both peered through it, seeing the nearest stumpy rotunda that confirmed they had reached the right place.

Stock looked around. "There must be a main entrance along here somewhere, and they would be daft not to have at least one guard." He stared for half a minute. "Not one that I can see, though."

"Perhaps it's a bit further along but we'd be in the open if we went down there. If that's a small shed I can see, that's where he'll be and all he has to do is look round and we're for it." Day's eyesight was obviously superior; Stock couldn't make out what he was talking about.

"Let's backtrack and try the other side."

The moon was now skitting in and out of the breaking clouds as they made their way back up the alley, revealing cats glaring back at them, daring them to cross their patch. One decided they had come too close for comfort and dashed under an ill-fitting garage door. Less than halfway there, but with the end in sight, they saw the outline of a sentry ponderously enter from the far end. Day took a lead from Stock as he disappeared into the more pronounced shadows of a path between two buildings.

It seemed an age while the sentry slowly paced towards them. Plainly, had other things on his mind as he took his time to continue past them. After all, he had no reason to suspect there was anyone else around. Another cat scurried across the sentry's path, following the first, and he made kissing noises in empathy.

All was silent other than the metallic crunching noise his boots made as he sauntered past them. Stock assumed he was patrolling the perimeter of the depot and it would take him quite a while to complete a full circuit. He didn't know how big it was but estimated they had at least five minutes before the sentry passed again, unless he doubled back.

Just before the guard disappeared round the corner, Stock realised why they had not gone further along the path: there was a series of triangular frameworks propped against the wall, effectively blocking further passage. Making sure the guard had gone, he shone his torch over them. He'd seen similar in England when he'd visited Whitstable. They were handmade frames for drying out fish. He got hold of one, tested its rigidity and decided it would do.

"Here, .drop the packs here and get the other end. We'll prop it up against the wall. You hold the bottom and I'll climb up first. Tie each end of the rope to each pack and we'll haul them up after. Forget the bolt cutters," he hissed.

Day was about to mention that the guard might find an errant piece of framework out of place when he next came round , but Stock already had hold of one end and was waiting for him to do likewise. It wasn't a ladder but it would have to do, and perhaps it wouldn't be noticed with all the other rubbish scattered about the alleyway. They set it so that it leaned into the wall. Stock hoped it would hold his weight as he stretched up for one of the ties that held it together and was grateful to feel Day's hand on the sole of his boot, pushing him up so that his body rested on top of the wall. A quick glance around to make sure they could get down the other side, then he reached down to take the iron bar that Day handed up to him along with the thin rope wrapped around their packs. Once Day had scrambled up to perch beside him, it took their combined strength to haul up the packs. The rope cut into their hands.

"Can you see what's down there? Daren't use the torches," Stock whispered.

"Not a thing," Day whispered back.

"Packs first. I'll hang onto the rope then lower you down."

Stock struggled to maintain his perch on the wall. He could feel every inch of the nine foot descent as he braced himself to counterbalance Day's weight, but it only lasted a moment before he released the corporal. He heard a curse from below.

"Clear?"

No reply.

"Clear?" A bit louder.

"Sort of."

Stock eased himself over the edge feet first and waited for the reassuring support form Day's hand which came almost immediately. He cursed. Bloody stinging nettles and brambles everywhere.

"Can't use the torches. Wait for that patch of cloud." He was looking up at the sky and saw that in a few moments the moon would do the job for them. As it did so, they saw they would just have to put up with being scratched and stung to get through the shoulder-high forest of viscous weeds for at least for the first ten feet or so. They hadn't donned their packs and carried them instead. Even so, it was far more difficult to make headway against the thorns and thistles than either of them had imagined. By the time they emerged into relatively clear space, they were out of breath again. Stock felt blood trickling down his face and wiped it from his eye.

"Bloody hell! Remind me never to go blackberry picking again," commented Day. Stock ignored him. He was surveying the scene in front of them. It was much as Longton had described and, as he had feared, only more confusing without the help of daylight. The occasional appearance of the moon glinting off the roundness of almost everything did little to help. One thing was clear, though; they would not be making their escape back over that wall. When this lot went bang, he wanted to be as far away on the other side of it as possible. He looked at the luminous hands on his watch and was pleasantly surprised to see they were actually on time so far. But he had a sinking feeling that it would take longer than had been allowed for to place the charges in the right place. Much as he tried to imagine the layout, he couldn't. All they could do was follow the decision they had made on the way over in the MTB: first locate the pipes that went to and from the quayside.

"Packs on but loosen the straps so we can get the charges out. We'll aim for the far corner on the right but mind your head on those pipes. Follow me and keep an eye out for any other guards."

After just a few steps, their first obstacle appeared in the form of a storm gully. It was only a couple of feet wide, but Stock nearly fell into it so they waited for the moon to make its appearance again before leaping across it. He remembered Longton's advice on firing the one furthest up the hill first but decided to leave that one until last.

Their second obstacle was a pair of large pipes, one on top of the other and spaced a few inches apart; too close to the ground to go under but high enough so they could not go over. Following them, Stock led them to their right. Before he knew it, the upper pipe had turned towards the middle of the depot, allowing them to belly flop over the lower one. Across the space between they could clearly see the main entrance and guard hut, the latter dimly lit from within. Despite the distance, the illumination from the far side of the quay allowed them to see that there was a pair of tall, meshed gates which were closed and probably locked. Stock was grateful he hadn't wasted their time investigating that way in. He had to assume that if there was more than one guard they would be on the outside of the compound. Day followed him across the open space towards the bulbous shape of one of the circular storage tanks and joined him in its deeper shadow; well aware that there was little either of them could do about the crunch that came with each footfall.

"Help me off with my pack, I'm going for a recce. You stay here," Stock ordered.

In Stock's absence, Day looked around but there was little to see in the blackness. Apart from the entrance, he could only make out another round tank beyond the one he was leaning against. Several minutes went by before he heard Stock returning well before he saw him.

"All ok?"

"Quiet here, sir, but I heard you quite a way away. Maybe we should have put socks on the outside of our boots."

"No time for that now. Anyway, I think the place is deserted. There are only one or two sentries and they're on the outside. I think

I have found the pipes that go towards the docks, and they must have controlling valves. Difficult to see them in this light but they come from a low tank on the far side. I will set those charges. Just behind this tank there is another and next to that a few pipes that come together with plenty of valves. You set those and meet me back here in five minutes."

"When do we set the timers?"

Stock thought about this for a moment. "Let's set them all at maximum now and they'll all go off at the same time. I'm going to keep one back for the wall at the top end so we can get out plus another two in case we find where they keep the drums. Here, off with your pack!"

In less than three minutes with Stock holding his hooded torch, they had separated the armed explosives which they put in one pack and the three unarmed ones in another. Before Stock disappeared again carrying the armed pack, he checked his watch noting that they now had less than half an hour to escape the compound. He had also left two of the armed ones with Day to place and prayed he would not run into any difficulty. He had every confidence in himself, even though this was his first time handling such an item and hoped Day would also rise to the challenge. He thought he would be able to find his way back to where the big pipes met the low tank easily enough but discovered that the darkness disorientated him. It was only when he almost bumped into it that he realised he had reached his destination. He looked up at the sky and hoped the moon would come to his aid but there was no sign of it anywhere. Feeling his way along the side of the tank, he paced the few steps to the big shut-off valves. So as not to make any noise, he placed the bar gently at his feet and let the pack slide off his back, took another half pace forwards and felt for the wheel he knew was there. It wasn't.

'This is no bloody good,' he thought to himself and got out his torch which he hooded as much as he could with his hand. It ruined his night sight again, but he could see both the wheel and the safety lever. Now he had his bearings, he switched it off and remembered

Longton's instructions for turning the wheel. In the brief time his torch had been on, he had seen that there was a second wheel on a parallel pipe just behind the first, but it was more difficult to get to so decided to concentrate on the one in front of him.

Putting both hands firmly on the wheel he tried to turn it clockwise. It wouldn't budge. He felt down and placed the bar interlocking the lugs with the spokes and tried again. Without too much effort, it moved, just enough so he could start to release the locking lever. I too was stuck. However much he heaved, it wouldn't move. He ended up kicking it. Still no movement.

He climbed over and tried the same manoeuvres again on the second wheel. This time it moved without him having to use the bar. He felt for the lever and found that this too moved without much effort. Ha to be the one that was in regular use, not the first. Now that the lever was out of the way, he turned the wheel anti-clockwise to open the valve and nearly jumped out of his skin when it let out a loud rusty squeal before it had rotated even half a turn. He instinctively stopped turning and looked around to see if anyone was looking at him and then berated himself for being so stupid. Nobody was going to see him in the pitch black, but everybody would have heard the metallic screech. There was no other option than to continue turning the wheel. He braced himself for another ear-splitting screech as he heaved.

It was a bit stiffer, but it turned almost three quarters before letting out another high-pitched screech. As he started to rotate it more freely, he heard and felt the flow of liquid from the tank passing through the opening aperture. He kept turning. With every rotation came the inevitable squeal of metal on metal. He lost count after six full turns. Tying on the charge proved a further challenge even though it should have been no harder than tying shoelaces, which he had done countless times in his life, although usually with the help of some light. In the pitch dark it was a different matter. The cord ends seemed to escape his fingers and knotted themselves back on to each other, and so the second charge he just lay on top of the pipe next to the spindle. Wherever the guard or guards were, along with anyone else who may be nearby, they would surely have heard him by now and would soon come running. He collected his pack before heading back towards where Day should have been.

As he approached their meeting point, he nearly tripped over an errant bramble that caught his foot and had to call for Day as he couldn't see him. He was rewarded with Day's response off to his right behind the first tank, "That's let the cat out of the bag. It sounded like a company of bagpipes warming up from here and I think our sentries heard it. Listen…"

Stock stood still following Day's suggestion. They could hear feet pounding along on the other side of the wall accompanied by loud voices. Torches shone through the meshed gates. It was too far for the beam of the torches to reach them, but they inched back behind the tank just in case.

"It's not going to take them long to bring help, so let's get going but stay behind this tank. We'll head for the wall in the far corner and look out for those drums. Follow me," Stock virtually mouthed the words.

From the faint light that emanated from the far side of the quay through the gates, they saw their way was blocked by a series of pipes stacked on top of each other. They found themselves heading further and further to their left towards the wall that they had climbed over. Stock was just beginning to consider using the rope to haul themselves over the top pipe when the bottom pair disappeared underground. He veered off to the right towards the rear wall, noting that the ground had started to rise just a little. Perhaps they would find a pile of drums that would empty their inflammable content in the right direction. His prayers were answered: stacked almost against the top wall were the drums they had been looking for, and considerably more of them than they had been expecting to boot. He took a hard look towards the gates from behind a vertical pipe. They were now almost a quarter of a mile away. Sure the sentries were still the other side of it, he took out his torch and retrieved the last three charges from Day's pack. A glance at his watch told him they had about ten minutes left. He set the timers for six minutes, three clicks each.

"Set for six minutes. Put this one in the middle of that lot. I'll put these two against the wall over there. See you there in one minute. Go!"

One minute later Day joined him. "Where now?"

"Behind that blockhouse." A small single storey square structure lay some fifty yards to their right. Just as they were disappearing behind it, they saw that someone had found the key to open the gates. A jeep type vehicle was entering the depot. It circled more than once before stopping, its lights casting long shadows in every direction, and they could see the outline of torch-bearing soldiers running, some in their direction. Stock looked at his watch, wishing he had set the last timers to just four minutes as it wouldn't take more than two for those soldiers to reach their hideaway, but he needn't have worried.

BANG! Followed by another explosion almost in the same instance. The nearest drums against the wall exploded, hurling bricks and concrete past their shelter, buffeting the air as it did so. Stock wanted to look round the corner and see if it had made a big enough gap in the wall but waited just a moment and was grateful that he had. BANG! the third charge went off, tearing holes in the thin skins of the drums and releasing the petroleum that had been manmade for just one purpose - to ignite.

It would have taken just blast to set the others off. With several pounds of explosive, the force proved great enough to set several dozen off all at once. The simultaneous ignition of thousands of gallons of the highly volatile fuel produced an immediate explosion, creating a blast wave that would have been felt a few hundred feet away. The fumes of the spirit hungrily sought out more air.

Savage blasts passed each side of the blockhouse. Stock shouted at Day to open his mouth and lie on the ground just as a gale of fresh air in the opposite direction replaced the blast and was sucked into the maelstrom of fire and destruction, adding to the inferno. As it did so they felt the whoosh of more of the petroleum fumes happily fulfilling their purpose in life by instantly flaring into yellow and orange balls of fire. It was similar to the conflagration a few days earlier, only on a far greater scale. They had set off an unstoppable chain reaction as the intense heat expanded other drums to bursting point. Despite being in the lee of the blockhouse, a tidal wave of hot air swept around them, searing anything directly in its path. When Stock opened his eyes, no more than ten feet away was the remains of a flaming bramble. Neither of them was counting and they only raised their heads when the crescendo lessened a little. To his horror, Day saw a flaming drum was trundling inexorably in their direction.

"Quick, out of the way." He half-pulled Stock to his feet and dragged him round the corner. They in full view of anyone looking from the direction of the gates, but it was unlikely that anyone would notice them as there was so much else to look at, even less so when one of the initial charges Stock had laid went off. Despite it being some two hundred yards away, they felt its blast as they pressed themselves into the brick wall of the blockhouse to avoid the flying drums that continued to rain down over a wide area. The assault on their senses was intense, not just from the noise that hurt their eardrums, but from the heat that ebbed and flowed with each explosion. Coupled with the mixed stench of incineration, it was almost enough to debilitate them. The staccato hail of exploding drums being torn apart from within, their irregular trajectories lacerating anything in their path that wasn't made of brick or stone, made this a very dangerous place to be.

Stock noticed that the gully they had nearly fallen into earlier was now a river of fire and flowing downhill towards the bottom of the depot, seeking out anything else that was vaguely flammable. He was not worried about the enemy; they were in more immediate danger of being caught by the unpredictable drums that continued to fly off in all directions. Still, it was time to get to the other side of the wall where at least they wouldn't be in the direct path of anything airborne, unless it came down directly from above. To his relief, the twin charges he had placed against the wall had brought down a section almost fifty feet wide. It was perilously close to what was left of the drums.

"Come on, time we were out of here. Let's go!." He had to nudge Day and repeat the order.

The beckoning gap was only a couple of hundred feet away across a relatively open space now strewn with all kinds of debris including flaming and twisted shells of drums which made it difficult to pick their way towards it. Before they could reach their destination, two things happened at once. A series of drums decided now was the time to explode and one sailed through the air before bouncing off the wall to their left and showering the area ahead of them in flames, which made direct passage impassable. Like a bowling ball coursing down its alley, what was left of one drum was heading straight for them.

Neither man had a chance to react to its speed as it passed between them. Stock felt a whack to his mouth and immediately tasted the saltiness of his blood, but he didn't fall down. Day toppled over, breathless from a flying glance to his midriff, and writhed on the ground in agony. Stock leaned over and pulled him to his feet and led him towards the gap in the wall. Their injuries prevented them from noticing the second thing that happened - Day's charges went off but not quite simultaneously and they felt the effect on their backs.

A real sense of urgency swept through Stock as more drums added themselves to the havoc that was close to engulfing them. At last, he managed to help Day over the rubble that was once the base of the wall, and he quickly led them along it a few feet and leaned against it.

Day doubled over and coughed like a forty-a-day trooper for a few moments but then stood up, wincing as he did so, still supporting himself with his back to the wall. They both jumped as the wall vibrated violently in reaction to another explosion and a piece of masonry was blow off the top and landed across the street. Only then did they notice that the buildings in front of them were on fire. In the eerie flickering shadows, Day saw Stock's face was a mask of blood and he smacked out an ember that was smouldering on his epaulette.

"Better get going, sir. This doesn't look too healthy either," Day gasped. But there was no reaction from Stock, so Day grabbed him by the elbow and guided him down the street, keeping the high wall on their left between them and the inferno beyond. After a few steps, Stock stopped and removed Day's hand.

"I'm alright now, thanks, Corporal. Just had to stop for a moment."

"It's this way. I recognise our alley over there."

"Eh?"

"This way."

Stock looked up and saw that they were approaching the top corner of the depot and knew they needed to turn right into the street that would lead them back the way they had come earlier. To get there, they would have to run the gauntlet of fire that rained down off the roofs of the warehouse on their right that ran parallel with the wall. He regretted his assumption that the wall would be their saviour.

A deeper sounding boom from within the depot shook the ground almost as much as the air, rattling loose more masonry on both the building and wall. With it came a brighter yellow light, sharpening the already dancing shadows around them. The section of wall that they had been leaning against a few moments before collapsed. Covering their heads with their arms, they ran the gauntlet regardless of what was coming at them from any direction, turned the corner and found that onlookers were emerging from their houses and had started to gather in small groups and convenient points. Most of them resembled an audience at a firework display. Although Stock and Day could clearly make out their individual features lit by the inferno as they stared at the conflagration, all the bystanders could see of them was two shadows, quite naturally running away from it.

They sprinted up the steepening hill away from what had become an arena of death. Only when they cleared the last house did they slow down and eventually stop. Breathless, they collapsed on the ground not too far from where they had encountered the goat, gasping for clean air. It was over a minute before they turned to look down on the scene that compared to a well stoked satanic pit spitting flame and smoke. They could feel the heat even from that distance and Stock had a fleeting feeling of sorrow for those inhabitants of Dieppe who lived nearby.

Day spoke first looking at Stock's bloody face in the flickering light, "Blimey, that was something else. Now I know how you felt back in Frévent."

"What?"

"I said now I know how you felt back in Frévent," Day raised his voice.

"That was nothing like Frévent - more like the gates of hell. We're bloody lucky we're not lying down there being roasted to death. There must have been an underground tank in that lot somewhere."

"What did you say, sir?"

"I said we're bloody lucky to be alive."

They stood up and gazed in awe at the fiery scene. "Looks like you turned the right valve. The water's on fire down by that ship."

Yellow flames belched black smoke obscuring the arc lights on the far side of the harbour which, by comparison, were just tiny pinpricks of light. Stock went for his binoculars and remembered that somewhere along the line he had discarded his backpack. He looked down at his watch instead, only to be disappointed to see that its face was smashed. He had no idea of the time.

"Come on, time to catch our ferry."

"Say again."

"Let's get our ferry."

"Right you are, sir. I don't fancy being caught by the Jerries after what we've done."

Stock shouted back at Day, "It's not the Jerries I'm worried about, it's the locals. By the look of things, we've set fire to this side of the town."

Before they crested the rise, they both glanced back and saw that the fire was spreading. Even when they were out of the direct line of sight, they could hear the occasional muffled explosion. Darkness took over in the shadow of the hill. Stock realised that he no longer had his torch either, but Day produced his and handed it to Stock who was grateful that it still worked. He flashed the arranged signal several times before they started their descent down the cliff path, no longer concerned or hardly caring about any patrolling sentries, and let its beam guide them down to the beach.

It was only as they stopped by the lapping waves that Stock noticed a ringing in his head. "Can you hear anything?" he asked Day.

Day wasn't paying attention but was looking out to sea.

"I said, can you hear anything?" Stock said in a louder voice, and briefly flashed the torch in Day's direction to get his attention.

"Not much. You sound a bit muffled."

"So do you."

Stock shone the torch at the breaking waves and realised he couldn't hear them. Day picked up on the significance.

"Must have burst our eardrums."

"If you say so. Keep a lookout behind us, will you?"

Stock resumed his tell-tale flashing out to sea in the general direction Ruddock had suggested. As he did so, he thought he felt the first spots of rain. Without the aid of a watch and with their frantic efforts, he had lost all track of time, but the mere fact that it was still pretty black out to sea indicated that dawn was still some way off. Ruddock would still be on station, so he started counting off seconds in his head and reset his mental clock every three hundred; five minutes. He reckoned it was about a quarter of an hour before the raft silently appeared not more than twenty feet away.

Stock mused that it was ironic that his feet were just about drying out at a time when he would have to get them wet again. They waded into the surf, rolled over the edge of the raft, and fell into the soft bottom. Not a word was said, at least none that either of them could hear, as the oarsmen sculled into the pitching sea that was rougher now than it had been a few hours earlier. The attention of all on board was held by the flames that reached up and illuminated the underside of the clouds in a bright orange glow. Coupled with a thick pall of smoke that was being blown away from them and the occasional flash that indicated that the flames were still finding intact drums, it was a sight nobody aboard had seen before, and the mesmerising effect distracted them from what they ought to have been doing. Stock thought it was about time to check they were heading for their rendezvous and turned around to signal again but before he brought his torch up, he felt a bump as the raft nudged the MTB.

Stock and Day had hardly sat down on the cabin bench before the throttles were opened and the boat surged forward. One of the ratings produced a wet but clean rag and handed it to Stock, mouthing something about his face. Stock realised it was so that he could wipe the dried blood from it. All the while, they could hear muffled orders over the droning engines and the thumping of waves against the bows but couldn't understand them as the ringing in their ears persisted. So for a while they just sat there reflecting upon the success of their deeds.

Instead of the boat maintaining just one direct heading, they felt it turn first to starboard, then port. Something had to be amiss. Stock decided to investigate, went through the cabin doorway and up the metal stairway to the bridge. In weak red light that came from the dials in front of the wheel, he could see Ruddock steadying himself in one corner while looking through his binoculars off to their left. Heavy seas were limiting their speed and spray regularly exploded from the bows only to be blown away by the strong westerly wind.

"What's up?" Stock asked.

Ruddock lowered his glasses before replying, "There's an E-boat following us, probably one of those two we saw earlier. What I'm worried about is his mate - I can't see him anywhere."

"You will have to speak up. I cannot hear much," Stock returned.

Ruddock repeated his observations a bit more loudly, adding, "Here, have a look if you like but I'll be surprised if you can see anything."

He moved out of the way so Stock could wedge himself in the same corner to look. He didn't bother straining his eyes for long, however, as there was an obvious art to maintaining a steady view on any given point from a bucking boat and, after his endeavours, it was proving impossible. He handed the binoculars back.

"Thanks," Ruddock grunted and then looked down at the back of the boat. One of the ratings was scanning with binoculars off to their left. Then he lowered them and shouted up at the bridge. "Red 100!" The port side was red and 100 meant the angle from their direction of travel, in degrees.

Ruddock immediately replaced Stock and peered through the glasses at the almost invisible horizon along the '100' radial. For almost half a minute he steadied his view and then swung his head around to almost directly behind them and stared for another few seconds before lowering his glasses and addressing the helmsman, "Maintain 305."

"How far?" enquired Stock.

"Oh, too far away to bother us for the moment. It's always worth bearing in mind that those E-boats have a longer hull than us and in these rough seas may have a couple of knots on us, but I think we'll make it before we come into range. At least we won't have to worry about torpedoes in this weather but if they get close, I'll radio through to Bembridge on the Isle of Wight and see if our chaps can't give them a nasty surprise. At this speed I expect it will take us about an hour and a half before we come under our guns. By then, it'll be daylight. Look, you can see it's already lightening."

A thin white line just under the cloud on the horizon over their right shoulder heralded the onset of another day. Stock didn't know where Bembridge was and wasn't to know that there was a main communications base on the Eastern point of the diamond shaped

Isle of Wight, nor that they could direct heavy artillery fire from the three forts that barred the Solent to enemy shipping, but he did understand that the bigger the boat, the faster it could go through the water when the sea became rough.

Ruddock was peering through his binoculars at the E-boat almost directly behind them and ordered a course change to 315 but it was still too dark to pick out with the naked eye. In the distance he could still see an orange reflection of their night's work and a tinge of pride in a job well done touched him for a moment.

"They were probably berthed at Le Havre and received a radio call when your lot went up. It's about fifty miles further down the coast, so it's lucky you signalled when you did, otherwise we'd have been caught red-handed and we'd have had to leave you behind. Did you know you were exactly on time?

Stock asked him to repeat the question. Ruddock pulled him down nearer the dials and looked at his right ear. Blood was still oozing from it. Looks like you caught something in your ear," he shouted. "Get Gerard to look at it when you go below."

"Can't feel anything," Stock replied and probed his ear with a finger before deciding it was safer to wait until whatever he was standing on didn't move about quite so much.

"That was some explosion. The best firework display I've ever seen. We saw barrels shooting hundreds of feet in the air and exploding like rockets. Remind me to ask you to open our Guy Fawkes fete next year."

"It was bloody terrifying, that's what it was and no, thanks - I think I'll give Guy Fawkes a miss, if you don't mind."

Almost nonchalantly Ruddock raised his binoculars again and searched across an arc between the two E-boats. "You can make out their wake now so they're definitely getting closer but there's still plenty of time. Come back to 305 and increase revs by 200," he addressed the helmsman before readdressing Stock. "Just to keep them guessing. Why don't you go below, you look like you could do with a sit down. I'll let you know when we get near Bembridge. Isle of Wight to you."

Stock agreed and braced himself with his hands on well positioned rails as he made his way back into the cabin and told Day about the E-boats that were chasing them. Then he shouted at him to look into his ear with his torch.

"Can't see anything but in this light I could miss an elephant."

"How are you feeling?"

"Oh, apart from a few singed hairs and a bruised tummy, I'm fine but I'm going to need some new socks and boots. Look!" He held up one of his boots to display a melted sole with a hole more or less where the ball of the foot would have been. "Lucky we got our feet wet early on, eh, otherwise I might have toasted toes. Don't think they taste very nice."

Stock bent down and looked at his own soles while keeping his feet in them and saw that his also were in a similar condition, but without the hole. "Must have been that blast wave when we were lying down."

"Yeah, and I don't think I'll need a haircut for a while either," Day laughed and turned round so that Stock could see the back of his head which showed an erratic singed hairline. Stock felt his own in response but gave up; it could wait. It was too rough to even consider going to sleep and in any case, if those E-boats did catch up them, Stock preferred to be wide awake when they did.

A rating appeared at the door and spoke to the navigator-cum-radio operator who was sitting at his apparatus in the corner attending to his charts. A few minutes later, Ruddock appeared, sat down at the desk and wrote on a pad of paper, before handing it over. The operator played with his Morse key.

"Just alerting Bembridge. You won't know this, but we've got eleven-inch guns in the Solent Forts, and they've got a range nearly halfway across the Channel. Well, not quite half but a good way out, and we're just coming into range. They're only a couple of miles behind us now but their guns are useless at this speed, and I hope they don't know about Bembridge. I'm considering zig-zagging a bit just to reel them in a little. More chance of hitting them that way." Ruddock was obviously relishing the forthcoming prospect and grinning widely. "Come and have a look."

Although grey and overcast, it was nearly broad daylight, and they could clearly see the two E-boats line abreast behind them. Ahead of them, off the port bow, he could make out darker mass of the Isle of Wight.

"If they had any sense, they'd turn around, but fingers crossed."

The radio operator appeared. "Sir, Bembridge confirms your signal."

"Thank you and confirm our approach." Ruddock took up his binoculars again and peered forwards and to starboard. "Come 020. We'll lure them into thinking we're heading for Selsey before we head into The Solent, that way more than one fort can bring a bearing on them."

It was clear that neither Stock nor Day knew the layout, so Ruddock explained further, "Imagine you're on a cricket pitch and we're the fielder aiming for the stumps from, say, square leg. We're more likely to hit the stumps if we've got three of them to aim at rather than just one edge-on, and right now we're circling behind the bowler. In a few minutes we'll be at ninety degrees to all three and then we'll turn directly towards them. Quite simple really and I see they're still playing ball. See if we can't knock 'em for six, eh?"

The swell had tempered a little in the lee of the big island and the wind still whipped the top off the waves, but the boat was noticeably nimbler in the slightly calmer waters. They all looked behind them and could now make out the outline of individuals. Ruddock took one last look towards Selsey before giving his next command, "Steer 290."

The MTB dug in and turned ninety degrees to the left directly towards the three forts. "That one off to the left is called No Man's Land Fort and houses the bigger guns. This ought to be excellent target practice for them. Any moment now..." Ruddock was chuckling to himself and enjoying every moment and Stock saw him start to jiggle his legs in anticipation. He considered himself a fair judge of distance when on land and particularly across farmland, but estimating a distance across a monotonous sea was altogether different. He thought they were less than five miles from the line of forts that sat squat across the water between the Isle of Wight on their left and Portsmouth on their right.

Boom! They all heard it at the same time and look behind to see where the shell was going to land. But it was one of the E-boats that had fired at them, and a small spout of water erupted a good hundred yards behind them.

Ruddock didn't react but explained, "At this point I would normally alter course 5 degrees or so but I'd rather the enemy followed exactly on the same track to make it easier for our chaps in the forts.

Another boom from behind. Because they were looking directly at one of the pursuers, they saw a brief puff of smoke from their gun disappear in the wind. Their shell went much wider this time but hardly had the spray spurted upwards before they saw and heard that one of the forts had fired. A much bigger pair of shells displaced a considerably greater amount of water and showered the surrounding sea. Neither of the E-boats was hit and although the big shells landed at the correct distance, the commander of the battery had obviously not allowed enough for windage. Both E-boats sensibly broke off their pursuit and turned away from each other, but now the other forts were firing, and a series of shells flew over their heads and peppered the sea around them.

Ruddock ordered slow ahead and a change of course into the current that put them beam-on to the action and they watched as more shells harassed the retreating E-boats. Just one hit, even a glancing blow, from any one of the big shells would have been enough to obliterate either of them but the guns had been placed there to defend against far bigger ships and the relatively tiny targets that jinked this way and that was a bit of a tall order. Still, as Ruddock had pointed out, they made good target practice. Yet one of the near misses must have done some damage as one of them was clearly having steering problems. At first, it seemed to be turning back, then it slowed to almost a standstill. This was probably just what the land-based guns were waiting for, and it seemed that all forts now concentrated their fire on it as it wallowed in the swell. Then it was gone in a splintering explosion that scattered parts of it high into the air.

The entire crew had been on deck watching the spectacle and let out a great whooping cheer before the first piece of debris even reached its airborne zenith. Stock and Day were carried away in the euphoric celebrations and joined in the cheer that was repeated three or four times before Ruddock brought them back to order.

"Steer 110. 1500 revolutions. Advise Bembridge we're looking for survivors."

He put the binoculars up to his eyes and began searching, first of all for the other E-boat to ensure it wasn't going to turn about and interrupt their rescue. He was glad to see it was fading into the distance, and then he focused on the area where the other E-boat had been. Ever so slowly they circled the patch of sea clockwise but from the large area over which the small remains of the E-boat that floated, it was evident that there were not going to be any survivors.

An hour later they docked at their berth in Southampton.

Chapter 12
The Option

As they disembarked, the threat of rain subsided with the easing of the stiff wind as if in some way reflecting that the trials and tribulations of their recent tricky crossings were now at an end. It felt good to be standing on English soil once again. Even the cries of the circling gulls seemed to welcome them home.

This time there was no car waiting for them. Stock momentarily felt deflated. Surely the importance of their achievement should have merited a luxurious form of transport at the expense of the War Department? Then he rallied and beckoned a waiting taxi at the entrance gates. The disgruntled taxi driver begrudgingly produced a chit for Stock to sign outside the gates of HMS Sultan and drove off in a huff, annoyed at not getting a cash payment. T were directed back to the armourer's building by one of the sentries.

"Is that it?" asked the burly, bearded warrant officer.

"Oh no, I nearly forgot," replied Day as he pulled the torch from his jacket pocket.

"You mean to tell me you left everything else behind but these two pistols and a bleeding torch?" the man protested, taking one out of its holster and inspecting it. "At least you've left all the bullets. What about yours, sir?"

"Didn't fire it either. They all ran away when they saw us coming."

The sergeant was crossing through items on his clipboard quietly cursing under his breath as they left and backtracked to the Admiral's office. It seemed to be becoming a bit of a routine but on this occasion they were not offered a seat, and instead stood to attention in front of his desk. Admiral Godfrey was clearly not in a good mood and was muttering to himself as he closed a file and almost threw it down on the desk behind him.

"Well?" he looked up and stared at them. "I see you've come dressed for the occasion once again. Be brief, I'm due in London shortly."

Stock knew they could not be the reason for his moodiness and decided it was because he had to go to London. He considered it would be best if he did exactly as he was told.

"Job done, sir."

Godfrey waited for more. "Is that it?"

"Yes, sir. You did say be brief, sir." It was a cheeky reply, but Stock had already made up his mind.

Godfrey glowered at him. "Any casualties, other than your uniform again?"

"No, sir, but Lieutenant Commander Ruddock arranged for the sinking of an E-boat."

"Yes, I already know about that."

On shore, they had all heard the firing of the big guns, but Godfrey had been on the phone at the time and had one of his aides report back to him. "At least that's one item of good news I can tell the admiralty about. Correction, two pieces of good news. Do you think you completely destroyed the depot?"

Stock and Day briefly looked at each other as it was not a question they had considered. "I'd say so, even the river was on fire. We only just managed to escape incineration ourselves. It was impossible to gauge if every tank caught fire."

Godfrey kept them waiting while he made up his mind and looked over at the mantelpiece clock on the bookshelf. "Right, well done both of you. I'd like your full report by this evening, Captain. Corporal, wait outside while I have another word."

The door had hardly closed before Godfrey continued, "Time is precious and I've a train to catch so I'll get straight to the point. One of today's meetings at the admiralty is to discuss the establishment of a special unit of commandos to carry out disruptive raids on enemy installations, very similar to what you and your corporal achieved last night. This has been on the cards for some time, and we've got several people in mind who'll make up that small unit. After your successes last night, you certainly qualify, so I'd like to add your name to that list. I stress 'like' as it's going to be purely voluntary. If you put yourself forward, it'll mean a transfer away from your current regiment and more than likely you'll be dead or captured before the war's half over. Nothing less will be thought of you if you decline and it'll go no further, but it's your chance to make an impact not just from the war effort point of view, but it may well further your career."

Stock was stunned as Godfrey knew he would be. The admiral allowed him a few moments to consider his proposal. A few days ago, he was just a lowly second lieutenant in an average regiment of Royal Engineers and now, not only had he been promoted to captain, but he was being offered the opportunity to become involved with the creation of what purported to be an elite unit.

"I suppose you want my answer straight away, sir?" he asked.

"Indeed."

"Can you give me until tonight when I present my report?"

"Until tonight then. 20.00 hours, here." Godfrey looked at his clock again. "Good day, Captain. See my Wren on your way out. She'll issue you with your pass for tonight."

"Sir." He saluted, about turned and left.

The Wren interrupted her work and got up from her desk as he appeared. "The admiral asked me to prepare some documents for you and I've put them in an envelope. Probably best if you open them when you are alone."

A bemused Stock wondered if Godfrey had a crystal ball. "Does that include a pass for tonight?"

"It does."

He couldn't resist it. "You'll have to speak up a bit. I've burst an eardrum. Does he know exactly what everybody's doing round here?"

"Oh yes, he's already told me you'll be back here at 20.00 hours this evening to submit your report."

Taking the long buff envelope, for the first time he was face to face with her and could see that she had natural youthful beauty, enhanced by the smile that she offered. "Thank you. It must be quite worrying that he knows what you're going to do, even before you do it."

She looked around to see how much interest the other staff were taking in their conversation and dismissed their potential intrusion as they were all busy. "Oh, we got used to it months ago and it's rather reassuring really."

"I'm not sure if I'd prefer to know what's coming next or wait and see. It would spoil the excitement."

"From what I've gathered, I think you've had enough excitement just lately. Did you manage to blow up the entire depot?"

"Oh, yes, well and truly, and got a bit singed for our troubles."

"Well, congratulations. I expect he'll be over the moon about that."

"If that's his way of showing he's over the moon, I'd hate to be near him with things go wrong."

Oh, don't mind him, he's just trying to do what's best for all of us and he hates failure." She leaned a little nearer and whispered loudly into his ear, "If you've got a favour to ask, now's the time - when he's pleased with you."

Stock mused that it was a little late for her to be telling him that and was about to tell her so when a muted shout from behind the door galvanised her into action and she went to enter Godfrey's office.

"By the way, what's your name?" he asked.

"Fisher." She flashed him a wide smile while putting her hand on the door handle. "The number here's Pompey 2884."

It was only when he and Corporal Day were walking back towards the ferry that would take them across the narrow waterway to The Keppel's Head, did he start to feel the effects of the previous night and realised he had lacked female company for some weeks. His proximity to Fisher - he didn't even know her first name, and right now, couldn't even recall her rank - must have jogged some primeval instinct within, but he also recognised that the foremost thing on his mind was rest. While their walk down to the water's edge did something to ease his aching muscles, he could feel a wave of tiredness creeping over the horizon. Before entering his room, he had told Day to meet him in the hotel lounge at 08.00 the following morning which would give them both plenty of time to catch up.

Before he undressed, he sat down next to the small desk and upended the envelope onto it. Some of its paired contents he recognised were for both him and Day, such as permits, passes, ID booklets and two one-pound notes as well as requisition slips for new complete kit to be presented to the quartermaster. There was also a smaller sealed envelope with his name on the front, marked 'Confidential.' He played with it in his hands, trying to decide whether or not to open it before retiring, suspecting that it had something to do with Godfrey's offer and concluded that if he did open it, his fate would be sealed for the rest of the war.

He stared at the faded blue roses on the wallpaper, hoping to find inspiration but instead found himself criticising his initial decision to volunteer for the Royal Engineers instead of his other choice of one of the artillery regiments. On balance, he had chosen an engineering-based regiment deciding that that was where his talents would be better utilised. Up until recently, this had proved to be the case. Construction as opposed to destruction.

He wondered again, for the thousandth time, if he could actually bring himself to kill someone when ordered to do so. He had previously made up his mind that he could if it served his King and country, but what if Godfrey's proposal entailed something more sinister and what would his own reaction be to carrying out orders that may or may not make sense at the time? Would his indecision cost him his life, and worse still, the lives of those around him? What would his father do? He was a bull of a man and had told him on several occasions how, when in the 17th Lancers during the first Boer war, they had charged a line of Africans on horseback, and he had gored several men with his lance. "You have to thrust firmly, otherwise you just end up wounding the buggers. And you can't let them live as they just get up again and throw a spear at you. Kill. You have to kill and kill cleanly," he had said.

Stock felt his head dropping towards the desk and managed to catch himself in time before hitting it. As he sleepwalked into bed, he realised he still hadn't opened the small envelope. He hadn't made up his mind whether or not he was going to accept Godfrey's offer and tried to imagine the decision as a set of scales in which he weighed it against what he already had, but then changed his mind and decided a pair of forest tracks would be a more appropriate analogy. Giant fir trees surrounded his path that forked directly in front of him, one going up and the other down. He altered the image so that they both sloped gently uphill and disappeared over a rise in the ground. One represented Godfrey's offer and the other his future with the Royal Engineers but both disappeared beyond his vision. He took the left path which he had nominated as Godfrey's and immediately recognised noises from creatures hidden behind the thickening trees. They were egging him on and talking amongst themselves, or were they laughing at him? Fallen pine needles deepened and impeded his progress and, just as he was about to give up, he was faced with a sheer rocky cliff with nothing to help him climb it but a grubby piece of brown string that dangled from above. A dead end then.

He reset himself back to the fork and took the right-hand path. This time the forest thinned to oak trees that filtered dappled sunlight onto a firm but grassy track and opened further onto a meadow. There in the middle stood a proud stag with breath snorting from his nostrils and staring directly at him. In the distance stood a homely looking hamlet, just the sort of place where he might want to live. But now the stag was charging and challenging him to either run or be gored. He looked round and knew he would never be able to reach the nearest tree in time. He reached into his pocket and produced a single sugar lump which he held out in front of him on his flat hand and watched as the stag turned into a fawn and nibbled at it. BANG! A shot rang out, followed by others, and the fawn vanished in a flash. More bangs but he couldn't see where the shots were coming from. Bang, bang, bang.

"Blimey, I thought you were dead." The landlord was shaking him awake. "Have you gone deaf or something? Been banging on your door for ages."

Stock jerked upright and peered from behind bleary eyes at an egg-stained tie that dangled close to him and thought briefly about using it as a bell pull.

"Are you alright?"

"Ok, ok, I'm fine."

"How about a thank you?

"Thank you."

"It's just gone 2 o'clock."

God but it felt like he'd been asleep for only a moment and as far as he could tell, every muscle in his body ached in one way or another, even more so as he put his feet on the carpeted floor. He'd wanted more time to sleep but he could hardly present himself to Godfrey, or anyone else for that matter, with his uniform looking the way that it did. Besides which, it was the wrong uniform anyway and it reeked. He only nicked himself twice as he shaved, using the borrowed razor the landlord had left him, and took a moment to reflect upon himself in the mirror. He thought he could see the first signs of laughter lines creasing the edges of his eyes. 'Better that than a double chin' he thought.

An uncertain quartermaster looked him up and down again and back to the requisition slip he held in his hand as it had been only two days ago since his last visit. "You'd better go through and see Captain Williams."

Stock had used his officer's status and jumped the lengthy queue and was now being ushered round the side of the wooden barrier and across the vastness of the high building towards a small office along one side.

"A Captain Stock to see you, sir. He has an, er, unusual request." The quartermaster placed the requisition slip on the desk.

A decently moustached captain looked up from his desk. "Right-o, ask him to come in will you, Sergeant." Stock thought he wouldn't be out of place at an RAF base as his whole demeanour suggested the typical optimistic outlook that went with those sorts.

"Now, let's see how we can please the Royal Navy yet again at incredibly short notice." He picked up the slip and frowned when he read the issue statement, looked at Stock and back again, much like the sergeant had done a few moments ago.

"Um. Bit out of the ordinary, this one. You are dressed up in a navy lieutenant's garb and this says you ought to be a captain in the Royal Engineers. Haven't too many of those around here I'm afraid but I expect we can oblige the sappers as well."

"It's a bit of a long story and I can't tell you much, but I expect you will have heard about the German E-boat that sank this morning."

By the look on his face, it was clear that he hadn't.

"Well, I was one of those on the MTB it was chasing."

"Still doesn't explain this slip does it? Umm? Don't mind if I check, do you?" It was not a question and he picked up the phone.

"I think you need to speak to Admiral Godfrey's department. A Lieutenant Fisher." He suddenly remembered her rank.

"Yes, I can see that from the stamp. Hello, can I speak to….."

The issue was resolved in less than a minute. An hour later, Stock walked out of the stores wearing his proper uniform, complete with kit and bag, and made his way back to The Keppel's Head where he would write his report for the admiral. Despite the underlying need for more sleep and rest for his aching muscles, he had a spring in his step and felt proud to be wearing the uniform of the regiment he had signed up to, although it was lacking the shoulder flashes that depicted his unit. The captain had wished him 'jolly good luck' in his own jovial way, and it brought a smile to Stock's face whenever he recalled that moment. What a happy fellow he was.

A good half an hour before his appointment with Godfrey, he handed over his report to another of Godfrey's lieutenants who immediately disappeared with it. From where he was in the ante room, he could hear the monotonous clacking from a typewriter. He had hoped to hand it directly to Lieutenant Fisher, but she was nowhere to be seen and he wondered if she was collecting him from the station. He started to picture her as the perfect woman, always dutifully on hand to fetch and carry, capable, not too condescending, active, happy with just the right sense of humour and, yes, beautiful, but then again not so much of a stunner that would attract unwarranted attention. The background clacking ceased, and it brought him back to the reality of his predicament. With horror he realised that in a few moments Godfrey would be putting him on the spot and all he had to go on was his gut instinct; and a crazy dream from a few hours ago.

With apprehension, he followed the lieutenant who ushered him into Godfrey's sanctum, sat down at an instruction and watched the admiral finish reading what he presumed to be his report. He was wrong. This time there was no greeting and Godfrey didn't offer any acknowledgement to his presence.

"Lieutenant-Commander Ruddock says here that you were nearly five minutes late back on the beach. How do you account for that?" Godfrey's challenging look belied a cheeky answer and one that Stock was not ready for. He thought he recalled Ruddock saying they had been on time but in truth he really didn't know, but perhaps this was another of Godfrey's double-edged questions that would help him determine a fuller picture of his attitude. If he blamed the dingy crew, anyone or anything else, or even Ruddock, then he might be considered as one of those who always 'passed the buck' but on the other hand if he took the responsibility himself, then he would have to broaden his shoulders.

"My watch face was damaged in one of the explosions and I had to guess the time," he replied steadily, not adding that it was an expensive Swiss one, a Longines.

His answer seemed to satisfy. "In that case I quite understand." It was a test then, and not a rebuke. "I only mention it since it was rather a close-run thing, what with that pair of E-boats suddenly appearing out of nowhere, but it all turned out rather well and it'll be something the press can trumpet. You mentioned that there may have been an underground storage unit in the depot. How did you arrive at that conclusion?"

Stock had thought about this one as he wrote his report and it made sense since there were several pipes that disappeared underground for no apparent reason, but he couldn't be sure. He told Godfrey as much, adding that in a confined space it wouldn't take much petroleum spirit to create a devastating explosion that would rip open any tank.

At last Godfrey smiled and closed the folder in front of him. "I think we can call this one an unqualified success due mainly to you and your corporal's expertise. You'll both be mentioned in despatches, at least. Now, what decision have you come to regarding the special unit being assembled? We're calling it the Special Boat Section."

This was it, then. It wasn't that he had been dreading it as he hadn't had enough time to, but he recognised the brief surge of trepidation and decided. He reached into his pocket, produced the unopened envelope, and placed it in front of Godfrey so that he could see that it hadn't been opened. He didn't say a word as the envelope said it all and he waited for Godfrey's reaction, which was a while in coming.

"It looks like the SBS is going to be devoid of a valuable member then?"

"I'm afraid so. You see I don't think I've got the do-or-die attitude that's obviously going to be called upon. I also rather think someone more qualified in handling boats would be better suited, so with my thanks, I must decline your offer."

"Nonsense," retorted Godfrey. "How do you know what you are qualified for until you try? Do you think the RAF asks someone if they can fly before they go up for the first time, or the Navy if someone can submerge before they go down in a submarine? No. So what makes you think you're not qualified? You've just proved yourself by destroying a valuable fuel depot behind enemy lines and I'll bet a pound to a penny you never realised you could do that a week ago. A man doesn't know his limitations until he has to."

Stock butted in, "And then it's too late."

Godfrey had more to say on the subject but didn't, as Stock's earlier comment about the do-or-die part now rang true.

"Very well then, but it's a pity I can't persuade you. In that case, you'd better open that envelope." He pointed and handed Stock a letter opener.

He unfolded the single sheet of paper that set out his orders and could hardly believe what he read. He was given an immediate two weeks leave after which he was to report to his unit now under the command of Lieutenant Colonel Alfredson at Hobbs Barracks, to assist in the construction of a nearby airfield at Horne in Surrey. It also confirmed his promotion to the rank of captain.

'The sly bugger,' thought Stock. He'd known all along that he would decline. "Why did you give me this envelope yesterday?"

"I'll let you work that out for yourself." Grinned Godfrey.

Chapter 13

In and Out

His friend had said it was only three miles and Stock needed a walk anyway. He was thoroughly enjoying the relatively slow stroll through the centre of London on a pleasantly warm summer's morning as it helped to clear away the muzziness from his head.

It was fortunate that a few days earlier, while waiting for a train on Platform 3 at Liverpool Street station, he had heard someone shout out his name and turned to see his friend, Hector Clements from his school days, striding towards him. It was even more fortunate that they were both heading for Norwich. For the next couple of hours, they swapped stories at a speed that would make any woman proud. Hector explained that, because of his qualifications and family connections, he had been seconded by the War Department's legal section and was now a KC in Blackman's Chambers in Lincoln's Inn. He was renting an apartment in Margaret Street, just off Oxford Street, and insisted that if Stock ever needed somewhere to stay, he was to look him up. A week later on his way back from Norwich, Stock did just that and they had both overindulged at Hector's club the night before.

As he nonchalantly diverted his route through a pleasant looking rectangular park and stepped smartly out of the way of a groundsman pushing a mower, he reflected on his week's visit to his family home in East Dereham, just outside Norwich. He hadn't phoned to say he was coming home as he wanted to see the look of delight on his mother's face as he walked through the door. He wasn't disappointed, but it was his sister who had skipped across the room first to give him a big hug. He was told he was going to be told absolutely everything that had been going on since he had left to enlist the previous year, and over the next few days he was led to one function or another, fete, meeting or whatever by his sister Jean, like a prize bull with a ring through its nose. His father was away in Scotland for most of the week to view prospective bulls for breeding and had been delayed at the auctions but, on the day Stock was due to leave, he appeared just in time to see him off and as usual had given him some parting advice when given the bare bones of his exploits in France.

"Thing big, always think big. You're a captain now so don't get bogged down with the menial tasks, and look further ahead than the next man," his father advised him.

Stock was already ahead of him. Without telling his family when he was actually due to report to his unit, he had decided to return a couple of days early, via his friend Hector in London. His route would have made a foraging ant proud since he had no map and couldn't remember the intricate details that Hector had tried to impress upon him the previous night, outlining the quickest way by dipping his finger into a glass of vintage port and drawing it out on a cloth napkin, interspersing it with crumbs of stilton to signify notable buildings. Stock half-wished he had kept that napkin, but from the shadows cast by the strong sunlight, he knew if he went East far enough, he would eventually come across City Road. Even if he didn't, he could always ask someone where the Honourable Artillery Company headquarters was. Before he caught the train to East Grinstead, he would carry out his promise to sergeant Angus Gritton. He had doubted whether the phone call he'd made to Lieutenant Fisher would come to anything, but she had said that she was accompanying the admiral to London that afternoon and would most likely be in town for a day or two and yes, if her duties permitted she may be available to go and see a show; she would ring him at his friend's, if and when she got the chance.

To a casual onlooker, his slow progress across the small grassy park may have looked out of place, considering most people in uniform were scurrying about on one errand or another, but Stock need time to clear his head of the excessive quantities of claret and port they had consumed and took his time, but was brought back to reality when he nearly got run over by a man on a delivery bicycle; only the tinkling of the bell had saved him.

He never knew how he managed it, but when he reached City Road and looked left, he saw the turreted building that housed the HAC. Pulling down his jacket so that it was straight, putting his shoulders back and assuming a military march through the gates, he strode up to the steps that led inside the impressive three-storey mini-castle. Off to the left of the foyer sat an elderly sergeant at his desk who immediately looked up and asked the reason for his visit, as only members and their guests were allowed any further. He then led him to an office on the opposite side of the hall where he was introduced to a Lieutenant Jenkinson in charge of the day's housekeeping.

"Captain Gritton, you say. That's captain Alec Gritton. Yes I know the fellow well. He's just been posted off to, well, I'd better not say. You know how it is these days." He was almost embarrassed at this last statement and looked down at his watch. "Look, it's just gone noon and I could do with some pep, would you like to join me in the Members Bar?"

Stock really wasn't feeling like anything smelling of alcohol but instinctively agreed. Once signed in as a visitor, he followed Jenkinson along a wide corridor that eventually led to a parquet floored lounge with double oak French windows opening out onto a perfectly cut lawn at the back. At the sight of Jenkinson's approaching, the barman reached for a bottle on one of the shelves behind the bar and began to jiggle it into a measuring cup.

"What's your poison, then?" Jenkinson wasn't to know that his comment touched a sensitive nerve somewhere in Stock's body. "I like to start the day with a pink gin. Find it helps sharpen up the taste buds on the tongue. Will you join me?"

"I'd love to." In reality he'd much rather down a pint of water but his pride, both personal and as an officer in the Royal Engineers, didn't permit it. He hadn't had pink gin for a long time, considering it to be very quick route to falling over. watched the barman as he carefully let drip two drops of the supposedly poisonous substance into a Paris goblet and expertly swill its contents round until it was smeared inside the entire glass. He then added a small quantity of crushed ice and delicately poured the large measure of Tanqueray gin over it. As he did so, an almost invisible mist of condensation filled the glass and evaporated over the rim.

"In or Out?" Jenkinson was referring to the addition of Angostura Bitters that only came in very small bottles and was the pink colouring behind the description of the cocktail. "I prefer mine in. Does wonders for hiccups when you have them."

"Out for me, please." Stock didn't need the addition of the intensely alcoholic medicine. And then it dawned on him. "By the way, I've heard this referred to as the 'In and Out' club. By any chance would that refer to the pink gins you serve here?"

This brought a wide smile from Jenkinson who was already halfway through his first one of the day hardly before Stock had had a chance to take a sip of his own. "I see you catch on quick old boy." He looked at Stock in an appreciating manner as one alcoholic recognising another but wasn't to know that his drinking companion wasn't one of those. "Some of us would like to say it is, as pink seems to be the drink at the moment, but there's stories about the real reason why." He leaned round and signed the chit offered to him by the barman, turned back to Stock and moved a little closer. "It's rumoured that the Earl of Grafton built this place in sixteen hundred and something for King Charles the First so that his mistresses had somewhere to stay not too far from The Tower, but far enough outside the walls of the City so as not to be clearly seen. Clever eh? But one particular mistress put herself about a bit, wasn't exclusive to Charles, and did her own bit of entertaining if you know what I mean. No sooner had one lover left than another would arrive. One in and one out. In and out." He paused to slurp his dwindling glass and pointed outside. "One day, the king found Grafton had got there before he had, and in a rage ordered his immediate beheading in the bedroom just above here and threw his head out of the window onto the lawn, and that small depression you can see just there is where it is supposed to have landed."

Stock looked outside at a small statue's base that was in an unnatural bowl on the otherwise flat lawn and was impressed with the story that had probably been blown out of proportion over the ages, but Jenkinson hadn't finished.

"Of course, there's one or two other stories floating about but that's what we like to tell the gullible. Personally, I think the real reason why it's called the In and Out is because there's a sign at the City Road end saying 'In', and the 'Out' sign is all the way over there on Bunhill. It's a short cut to The Artillery Arms. Anyway, you haven't come all this way just to sate your curiosity…"

"You mentioned Alec Gritton. How come you know him?"

"I don't but I came across his brother Angus in France last week and promised to drop in on his brother if I was passing. I'm afraid I may have some bad news as the last I saw of him, his tank was taking on some Jerry heavy artillery and I don't think he or his crew made it."

"That is bad news. Not sure I recall Angus, but was he about so high with wiry black hair?"

"That's him. Competent man from what little time I spent with him."

"I'll make a note in the register, but it'll take some time for that kind of info to come through, what with the evacuation mess. Shame really if that's the case as Alec's just been posted to North Africa and I gather they came from a Presbyterian family in, was it Perth?"

"Sounds about right. His Scottish accent was quite strong."

"Here, fancy some lunch?"

Stock wasn't sure if he did or not but took Jenkinson's offer as he might not dine again in such auspicious surroundings for quite some time. Before they sat down, they were joined by three other officers and made quite a lively circle. He finally left the HAC well into the afternoon feeling a lot better.

The loud ringing of Hector's phone on the small table right next to the armchair he was dozing in reminded him that his hearing had returned to normal. He jerked upright to answer it and was delighted to hear that it was Miss Fisher. Yes, she would be staying in London for the next few days and yes, she'd love to take him up on his offer of a show, perhaps one at the Criterion theatre. Could he pick her up in time for the evening performance? And by the way, her name was Mary. His heart soared at the prospect of seeing her again.

He almost sprang onto Margaret Street, not just looking but also feeling rather dapper, and marched towards Piccadilly Circus where he had arranged to meet Mary outside Lilywhites. He wasn't nervous as he had felt a natural affinity with her almost from the first time their paths had so briefly crossed. He had the impression that it was mutual. She had suggested that, since there was plenty of time, that they went for a drink in a nice pub round the corner called The Captain's Cabin, just off Jermyn Street.

"How did you find this place or are you a regular?" he asked as he handed her a tumbler of gin and tonic.

"My Uncle brought me here once when he was meeting some bigwig from the admiralty and thought I was old enough to get to know the more salubrious places hereabouts. He's dead now but I can still hear him: 'If you're going to get involved with those senior service chaps then you need to know where to stay out of trouble.'" She rather unsuccessfully attempted to mimic his baritone voice by lowering her own. She let out a small laugh in embarrassment. "He was a bit of a gruff man but knew his way round London and had a flat which I often stayed at. Oh, look. Peanuts. That man over there's got some peanuts. Oh, do try to get some for me, I adore them but can't get hold of them on the coast."

Stock looked round and saw a man dressed in RAF blue just taking a small bowl from the bar towards his alcove. "Give me a minute." He was back in two and her eyes eagerly followed the bowl as he teased her with it before he put it down in front of them. "I suppose I could nickname you Peanut."

"Don't you dare." Her eyes briefly flared. "Besides which I also like cashew nuts, but they make me sneeze. Cashew! Cashew! Like that." She imitated the sneezes. "So, you can't call me cashew either."

"Have you got any other names I can call you other than Mary?"

"You really don't know who I am, do you?"

"Yes I do. You're an unattached and very attractive young lady who works for a grumpy man in Portsmouth who likes to come to London a lot and, let me guess…Your uncle was a sea captain who used to import nuts and ended up behind a desk somewhere in the War Department and managed to get you a job, right?"

"Not close enough, but a fair guess and no, I am not telling you my middle name - at least not yet." She took a delicate sip to help wash down the few peanuts she had been munching on. "Keep trying and I'll let you know if you're getting warm."

Stock was relishing the game. "Alright then. You obviously have connections with the navy. From your accent, I would say your family lives in a large house somewhere in Hampshire. Not farmers though, more equestrian. You were educated at Cheltenham Ladies' College."

"Not close enough, except for the Ladies' College bit, and the equestrian part. You're right about those. Ok, I can see we'll be here all night, so I'll give you a clue. My grandfather had the nickname Jacky."

Stock could tell from her smug look that she was enjoying the cat-and-mouse game and he racked his brains to try and match her. He could tell that this was some sort of test and, if he passed, then he might get to see her again, but if not…How many men had the nickname Jacky? He could think of only one and double checked himself before answering. But then all the pieces came tumbling into place. He had been only nine years old when the man had been given a state funeral and remembered his own father telling the family what a great man he was. He tried not to look astounded.

"You are Admiral Jacky Fisher's granddaughter. That is how you have been appointed to Admiral Godfrey's staff."

"Correct! Here, you've won a peanut," she laughed, revealing a perfect set of teeth as she flicked one in his direction across the tabletop.

Stock was as impressed as any man ought to have been but didn't want to give her the satisfaction of seeing him impressed. Jacky Fisher had been the First Lord of the Admiralty when the Great War had broken out and had been responsible for creating Britain's fleet of dreadnought battleships that had purportedly saved England from invasion. He held his hand out and let her drop half a nut into it as his mind whirled with the thought of being in the company of the granddaughter of arguably England's second greatest seaman in history next to Nelson.

"Well, now, that is not all. In which case it looks like I have won my bet."

"Bet? What bet?" Her response was tetchy at the thought of being the object of a mere bet.

"I should stand to win, oh, let me see," he paused as if making a mental calculation. "Nearly a pound. Ought to cover at least part of this round."

"Just a pound! Exactly what is this bet?"

Stock was quite rightly gambling on the fact that she had a natural superiority complex, and had just about managed to undermine it, but he doubted he could keep up the charade for much longer. She seemed too intelligent for that. "Oh, it is just a standing wager we have in our regiment that whenever any of us come across a Wren and get to take them to the theatre, how long it will be before they tell us some cock-and-bull story about how famous their parents are, but in your case, my sergeant upped the odds as he reckoned you must have been just a stand in."

Her compressed lips said it all. He was just taking a swig from his glass when he felt a sharp pain in his left shin. She had scored a direct hit with her toe. "Ow…."

They sat there for a moment looking into each other's eyes.

"I supposed I deserved that."

"Yes, you did, but I see your point. After all, it's not every day one comes across a descendant of someone famous, which is why I don't go telling everybody the first chance I get. Well, almost." She lowered her eyes and took another sip and Stock waited until she looked at him again.

"Do not worry, your secret is safe with me. I promise not to bandy your name about. I expect that once people do find out about who you really are, you regret telling them. I cannot say the same about me as I am a comparable nobody."

"Oh, that's not true." Her retort carried real conviction. "I think you are wonderful, especially turning down the admiral's offer."

"I suppose you would know about that, being his private secretary. I feel that I let him down, but those are my convictions."

"Oh no, quite the reverse. He's very pleased with you and I think you made exactly the right decision. You see, I've seen men like you come and go and end up in a graveyard behind some unknown church somewhere in the middle of nowhere and I think they were trying to please him, but it always fails. You're the first person to stand up to him, which makes you more than a somebody."

"I suppose you know all about me from my file?"

"Well, er, yes, I did get a chance to look through it." By the time she had ashamedly lowered her eyes and raised them again, she saw Stock smiling. "Oh, do stop treating me like a child. Of course, I was going to look through your file. I look through everybody's file and, yes, I do know everything about you. Where and when you were born, your parents' first names, how many brothers and sisters you've got etcetera, etcetera. What do you expect me to do? It's my job, making sure that those who the admiral choses are the right sort."

Stock saw her hand resting on the table and put his over it. "Am I the right sort, then?"

"Yes." She felt an electric elation as their hands touched.

***

"Captain, eh? How on earth did you manage that one?" Stock had found Major Wavertree at the end of the runway at the airfield by the village of Horne near East Grinstead. He was inspecting the perimeter track that was bound by a line of oak trees. "Have to have some of these down if they want to land anything here bigger than a biplane here. Captain, now. You know how to jump the queue, don't you? Well, welcome back and just in time too. A few of us didn't make it back and that included Captain Wilby, so you'll be taking over his company. Here, how long do you think it'll take us to fell this lot?"

They continued along the line of trees towards a small pond at one end. The Major continued, "I've got a job for you, unless you want to delegate. Can you put together a block of toilets again?

www.ingramcontent.com/pod-product-compliance
Lightning Source LLC
Chambersburg PA
CBHW032224190726
48289CB00007BA/2381